READY TO BURN

MANDY MICHELLE

SCARSDALE PUBLISHING

TRADEMARK ACKNOWLEDGEMENT

Kit Kat

CHAPTER ONE

Ronan stirred his latest creation over the kitchen stove in Firehouse 3 and called, "Who wants chili?"

Lieutenant Keith Murphy stepped up, bowl in hand. "Always, McGuire."

Ronan poured a ladleful into his superior's dish and laughed when Keith nodded for a second helping.

The lieutenant tasted the chili then raised his brows. "This is the shit. Is this what you're going with for this year's chili cookoff?"

"Something like it," Ronan said. "I'm determined to beat the guys from Firehouse 4 this year."

"Well, whatever you're doing, keep it up, man."

Ronan grinned. "Glad to hear my cooking classes haven't been a waste of time." Attending culinary school between shifts had been a helluva challenge and didn't leave time for much of a social life, but he enjoyed it.

"Well, whatever you're doing, keep it up." The lieutenant stuffed a heaping spoonful into his mouth. "You excited for tonight, McGuire?"

Five more guys on shift filed in and Ronan filled another

bowl, tossed grated cheddar on top, and slid it down the counter to Mike Sheppard. "No, sir."

"Is our virgin nervous for his first time?" Mike grabbed the ladle from Ronan, heaped more chili atop the cheese, then dug in.

"You were the virgin last year, Sheppard." Diego Fuentes slapped Mike's back. "And if I remember correctly, pretty damn thin."

Ronan filled Diego's bowl. "Just how thin was he?"

Ronan filled three more bowls before getting his own, then joined the men at the table. He scooped up a spoonful of chili.

The fire alarm blared.

Ronan groaned. Happened every time.

Mike wolfed down another bite, then dropped the spoon with a clatter as Ronan twisted off the knobs on the stove. Both men turned in unison, hurried through the door, and took a quick left into the truck bay.

Ronan stepped into his turnout pants, slung on his jacket, and grabbed his helmet. He jumped through the truck's open side door as the lieutenant turned over the engine and flipped on the sirens.

Ronan, shoulder to shoulder with Rogers, bowed his head in a quick prayer. He took a deep breath to calm his pounding heart. Each call always felt like the first.

They pulled away from the firehouse. In less than three minutes, Ronan caught sight of black smoke rising into the sky from somewhere in a residential neighborhood to the west. The fire truck turned onto Westminster Road. The smoke seemed to come from one of the older homes behind Henderson Point.

Keith halted the truck in front of a two-story house where bright red flames lapped at the fresh winter air through the broken windows of a detached garage. Thick clouds of black smoke spiralled heavenward. The garage siding had begun to melt and blacken. The flames hadn't spread to the house. Yet. The house sat only twenty feet from the garage and could catch in a matter of minutes.

Half the neighborhood stood across the street with phones outstretched to record the action.

"We're going to be online, again," Diego muttered. "Look sharp out there, guys."

"Diego and Sheppard on hose," the lieutenant ordered. "Peters, clear the house. McGuire and I will secure the perimeter."

The men sprang into action.

"Fire Department." Ronan jogged across the street toward the onlookers. "Anyone inside?"

"Manny's away on a big demolition job," someone said.

"Away?" Ronan blurted.

A man nodded. "Manny owns J & M Demolition and they have a big job down south. He lives alone, so no one's in the house."

Ronan whirled and called "Thanks!" over his shoulder as he hurried back across the street toward the fire truck.

Water arced from the hose of the deck gun that Mike and Diego directed at the garage. Billows of white steam poured from the garage as water hit the flames. Ronan teamed with the lieutenant to pull a hose from the truck. In seconds, they had a stream of water directed at the doorway. With a bang, the door blew back on its hinges and slammed against the wall of the garage. Onlookers screamed.

The heat, God, that heat seeped through Ronan's protective gear and into his body. Sweat rolled down his back as he widened his stance to brace against the pressure of the water and directed the heavy stream to douse the flames. Others on the team used hand lines to wet down the home, fences, and the neighbor's garage to keep the fire from spreading.

Hours later, they had the fire controlled. Diego strode to the right side of the garage with a halogen—a crowbar on steroids—and fitted the end into a crack in the wall and pulled back the siding. Oxygen-fueled embers burst into flames. Diego threw up an arm to protect his face and stumbled back several paces as Ronan sprayed water into the new access point.

Another long hour later, they had the fire extinguished and the lieutenant cut the water to Ronan's hose. The ache in his arms had gone numb from overuse. Ronan rolled his shoulders. An hour from now, the ache would return with a vengeance.

While the rest of the crew stowed gear, Ronan headed back to the garage. Today was December 31, two weeks to the day since the fire on Lenore Street, another house where the owner had been away when their home caught fire. This was the fourth fire in six weeks, each exactly two weeks apart, where the owners had been away. Well, the owner of the house on Hedge Lane had been home, but he'd returned a day earlier than expected and was asleep when his home's fire alarm went off. He'd gotten his wife and daughter out but had sustained burns to his arms and face.

The fire marshal would assess the damage and cause of the fire, but Ronan wanted to know if this fire was connected to the other three fires. The first had been a faulty gas line, the second, electrical, and the third, a can of lighter fluid that the fire marshal ruled that someone had slung through a garage window.

Separately, there was nothing connecting the fires. But the fact that the owners weren't home—or weren't supposed to be home—bugged Ronan. Not to mention, each fire had occurred exactly two weeks apart.

Ronan reached the garage and carefully stepped over debris that had fallen at the entrance. Blackened rubble of the half-walled, roofless structure crunched under his steel toe boots.

Everything inside the garage had burned. Ronan identified the remains of a melted plastic gas can on the property. As he started to turn away, he spotted what looked like a shattered beer bottle near the rear of the garage. He exited through the front door and strode around the garage to the glass. Ronan toed through the debris and found what he was looking for: the bottle cap. He rubbed the ash off the surface with his thumb and recognized the brand: Red Cap.

Keith joined him. "Not good, huh?"

Ronan rubbed his stiff neck. "No."

"The fire investigator is on her way." Keith shrugged. "Our work's done. Plus, you don't want to catch more flack for mucking up a fire scene."

Ronan grimaced. He wouldn't soon forget that stripping down from Fire Marshal Kate O'Malley last month. She might be a five-foot-nothing blonde, but she was no pushover. She'd probably love nothing more than to see him fired. She liked order, and he had a way of messing that up for her.

Ronan stared at the house. "Two weeks on the dot."

"Don't start," the lieutenant said.

"The fires are connected, Lieutenant. I feel it in my gut."

"We don't solve crimes, McGuire. We put out fires. You have a bigger problem, anyway."

Ronan frowned. "What's that?"

"A room full of rowdy women."

Ronan groaned and rubbed his face. Call him crazy, but he would rather investigate this fire than face a bar full of horny firemen groupies. Even if that investigation meant dealing with O'Malley.

A pair of hands landed hard on his shoulders and he smiled before he turned around. "Hey, Janis." Thank God those hands belonged to his favorite policewoman and not the fire marshal. This woman liked him.

"You went in, didn't you?" Her casual voice didn't fool him for a minute. "I told you to stick to your job and just put out the fires."

"That's exactly what I did, officer." He winked and flashed his most charming smile.

Her eyes narrowed. "You know what I mean."

He had known Detective Janis Rylands of the Rapid Falls Police Department since high school. They had dated during their sophomore year, back when she was Janis Simmons. She had married an accountant, of all people, and was happier than he had ever seen her. A hell of a lot more confident, too.

"This has me worried, Janis." He stared at her face and frowned. "You look a little green. You feeling okay?"

She grimaced. "Let's just say, morning sickness isn't just for mornings."

"You're pregnant?" Ronan grinned. "Congratulations. You're going to be a stellar mom."

She laughed then grimaced again. "Thanks. Don't spread the word around the firehall, okay? It's early."

"Done deal," Ronan said. "Be careful out here, huh?"

"I'm always careful, McGuire. And nice subject change."

He drew an x over his heart. "I promise not to set foot in another crime scene."

She laughed, which made her appear sixteen again. "You're such a bad liar. Oh, and have fun tonight with the ladies."

"I will."

She shook her head. "A damn bad liar."

CHAPTER TWO

ALISON APPROACHED ANDIE'S PUB AND, EVEN THROUGH the closed door, heard laughter and music. Another busy New Year's Eve. She entered and hurried to the bar where the owner, Joey, poured drinks and her boss, Megan, hoisted a full tray of cocktails over her shoulder.

"Thanks for coming in, Ali. We're swamped." Megan turned on her kitten heels and shook her shapely hips as she walked to a table of noisy women.

As the co-owner, Megan normally ran the numbers in her office, kept the stock room full, and juggled the schedule. But tonight called for all hands on deck.

Alison hurried to the office and put her purse and keys in the lower desk drawer before heading back to the bar. In her five years on staff, Alison had never seen Andie's so full. It was close to bursting at the seams—and with good reason.

Tonight was the big reveal of the Rapid Falls Firefighters Charity Calendar. Megan was lucky to have landed the exclusive event at her bar. The proceeds from calendar sales went to charity, but the drink sales were all Andie's. The best part, the tips belonged to the servers. Monday was Alison's usual night off, but with Roseanne out sick, Alison was quick to fill in. Huge profits could be made off the single and not-so-single ladies trying to catch the attention of sexy firemen. Throw a half-naked man in the room and, *voila*, the purse strings were loosened.

All the small pubs in town had rallied for the right to host the twelve sexy calendar boys. Meg's place had won out. The stage had been a major selling point, but the seating capacity had sealed the deal.

Besides the logistics, Megan deserved the honor. Not only had she built this place from the ground up while her husband served overseas, she'd managed to keep the doors open during Joey's six-month recovery at the veterans' hospital in the next town over. She was strong, brave, and one heck of a boss. A boss who had become Alison's best friend and biggest supporter.

Tonight, the firemen were volunteering their time, too. They were sweet to do this for charity. Heck, they probably didn't mind having their egos stroked, either. Most were probably hoping to go home with a big breasted consolation prize, so Alison doubted any of them would complain.

An eighty-something-year-old woman sitting at the nearest table to the left signaled her. Alison hurried to her table. "Hey, honey, I'll take another *Quick Fuck*."

Alison winced inwardly at the colorful cocktail name which was Megan's pride and joy. She and Joey had searched to the ends of the earth to find the most vulgar cocktail names for tonight's event. The couple were nothing if not dedicated.

"I'll be right back with that." Alison smiled, then headed back to the bar through the mass of bodies and howling laughter. She didn't even have her apron on yet. God, these women were wild with the promise of testosterone and a little chest hair.

"You look nauseous already, Ali." Joey winked a dark, chocolate-brown eye.

Meg's husband was such a damn comedian, and she loved him for it. She needed to laugh off her discomfort.

He twirled a bottle of vodka in that artful way only bartenders trained in the nineteen eighties could pull off. "What do you need, little lady?"

"I don't know why your cocktails have such ridiculous names." She rolled her eyes to distract attention from her blush.

"It is all because of you horny women, Ms. Walker. You keep us bartenders in business."

"A *Quick Fuck*," she said.

Joey laughed, and his eyes shone with mischief. "What was that, Ali? I couldn't hear you. It's so damn loud in here."

Alison reached over the marble bar for her black apron and tied it around her waist, all while skillfully avoiding Joey's eyes. "You heard me."

"Alison." Joey poured himself a shot of vodka. He slung it back, gave a satisfying "ahh," and slammed the glass down. "This stuff ain't cheap. I don't want to make the wrong drink." Another of his teasing winks accompanied his lecture.

God, she hated this man for making her say it out loud.

"Joey. I need a *Quick Fuck*."

Amidst Joey's laughter, a deep male voice behind her said, "Maybe I can help with that."

A warm hand pressed her lower back. Alison started at the heat that flashed through her. Oh, no. She couldn't let herself bask in the male attention sure to overflow tonight. She couldn't afford to. Not anymore.

"You wish," she shot back without looking at him.

He gave a low laugh, as if he did wish for it.

The heat headed south. Great. His warm, rich voice would

surely melt her butter. She wouldn't even get started on his delicious, husky laughter.

Alison whirled to tell the man to get lost, but her mouth went dry as her eyeline slammed into a tight, navy t-shirt stretched over muscled pecs. The Rapid Falls Fire Department logo left no mistake about who had propositioned her. One of the guests of honor. One of the men who had donated his New Year's Eve for the county's sick children.

She was a mother. He was a hero.

Alison bit her tongue. She couldn't be rude to a man who saved lives. Instead, she embarrassed herself by keeping her gaze on his chest and stammering, "It's...it's a cocktail."

Her pulse kicked up. What kind of cocktail waitress couldn't handle the word cocktail?

Alison faced the bar and said, "All right then. That's one *Quick Fuck* for me and one for the firefighter, please, Joey."

Without looking at his face, Alison turned on her tip-earning heels, a trick honed from years of practice, and headed for the table. She had a sweet baby girl at home who counted on these paychecks to keep her in diapers, cute onesies, and of course, adorable shoes. Like mother, like daughter.

The novelty clock on the wall told her she had four hours left until midnight. Four hours left to avoid flirtatious firefighters who made her question her decision to avoid men. She would have to look at the situation glass half full. Half full of a *Quick Fuck.*

CHAPTER THREE

"Christ." Ronan leaned back against the closed office door; the din of the bar now muted behind him.

Back in the safety of the small ten-by-ten office located in the far corner behind the bar and overcrowded with all twelve firefighters in varying states of undress, Ronan set a beer down on the desk in front of his lieutenant and took a drink of his *Quick Fuck*.

Keith took a long drink of his beer. "Struck out with the waitress, huh, buddy?"

"You saw that?" Ronan blew out a deep breath, thankful he hadn't inherited his sister's tendency to blush tomato red when teased. "Maybe. I don't think she's interested."

Keith lifted a brow. "Why not? There are three hundred women here who would do anything for your ass. Is she married?"

Ronan set his drink on the desk, then shoved his jeans off his hips, leaving him in nothing but his black t-shirt and boxer briefs. He slid into the turnout gear all the guys had agreed to wear for the New Year's Eve Calendar launch party.

"Nah. No ring. I think I offended her."

He winced inwardly at the memory of his earlier behavior. That damn line was right out of Mike's playbook. A book no man with any decency should be reading from. Hell, even his grandmother would have been disappointed.

Keith grinned. "You never could flirt."

Ronan laughed. "Neither can you. You're lucky Missy took pity on you and married you."

Keith pulled off his wedding ring and shoved it deep in his pocket. "I never denied the lucky part. If you're interested, Missy's sister still wants a piece of you."

Ronan grimaced. "Only a piece would be left after Angie finished with me."

Keith grunted a laugh. "You're probably right. Though it would be a pleasant way to go."

"I've heard wedding rings make you more attractive to the ladies." Ronan nodded at Keith's left hand.

"Exactly," Keith said. "It's why Missy wants me to take it off."

"Wait. Angie's still single?" Mike grabbed Ronan's drink from the desk and drained the glass.

Ronan pinned Mike with a mock stare. "Ass."

"Well, you didn't bring me a drink," Mike said. "Playing favorites with the lieutenant?"

"Maybe."

Always the peacekeeper, Keith said, "Go grab another shot, Ronan. We drink free tonight. That'll give you a second chance to hit on the waitress."

"Which waitress?" Mike peeked into the bar. The closest table of women screamed and waved. "Damn, those women are dangerous."

Ronan bit back a smile. The guys pretended to be such big shots with the ladies, but with the bar at capacity, some of them were intimidated. Himself included.

Mike nodded toward the door. "Beer, Ronan."

Ronan sighed. "It's not going to happen."

Mike waggled his brows. "If you don't want the waitress…"

Keith caught Mike's gaze. "Let it go. Ronan's interested."

Ronan shook his head. "You're a bunch of horny dogs. I'm here for the kids at the children's hospital. That's it."

"*Sure*, you are." Mike waggled his brows.

"How much longer before we get this over with?" A lot of the guys loved this stuff but, hell, he was a charity calendar virgin.

"Bunch of children. I'm not your mama," Keith said.

A knock sounded and a pretty redhead with curves in all the right places slipped into the office. "Hi, boys. Keith. I'm Megan Andrews. This is my bar."

The guys hooted and hollered.

She smiled. "Before the night gets too wild, I wanted to thank you all for giving up your New Year's Eve for the Rapid Falls Children's Hospital."

"It's our pleasure, ma'am," Ronan said.

"Suck up," Mike coughed, earning him a smack on the back of the head from Rogers.

Megan pushed onto her toes and pressed a kiss to Ronan's cheek, then patted his chest. "Oh. Are you all so hard?"

Mike laughed. "We are now."

Keith ducked his head, but Ronan glimpsed his smile.

Megan's eyes widened. "Um, I didn't mean that." She pressed her hands to her pink cheeks. "Don't tell my husband."

Mike winked. "Your secret is safe with us."

"Okay, boys." Megan's face glowed red. "I'm going to introduce you. Come on out when I call your name. We're going to play some games, get the ladies involved. Encourage them to buy your calendars. We'll take a few breaks throughout the evening for calendar signings. Oh, and I had an idea I need to run by you."

"Shoot," Keith said. "These guys will do just about anything."

She smiled. "I want to auction off a New Year's Eve Kiss. What do you think?"

Keith held up his hands. "I'm out. Married."

"Also out," Diego said.

Ronan looked over at Diego. Interesting. That man was usually down for the crazy.

"How about three volunteers?" Megan asked.

"I'm in." Mike, the obvious first volunteer.

Al Peters, the lifelong bachelor, was next to sign up.

"Ronan is also up for the challenge." Mike grinned. "He hasn't had a New Year's Eve kiss in years."

Ronan groaned.

The redhead looked up at him. "Will you?"

With those batting eyelashes and big blue eyes, he was certain she got everything she asked for.

He laughed. "Sure. Why not?"

Megan beamed. "Thank you, thank you. You ready to make a couple hundred ladies very, very happy?"

The guys cheered and the women outside the door responded in kind. Megan gave a little wave and slipped out the door.

"You look a little green, Ronan," Keith said when the door clicked shut behind Megan. "I know you're new at this, but you can handle it. Just flash those dimples. They'll love you just like all the women you rescue."

Ronan nodded. It was no secret that the hours he spent in the gym had earned him quite a fanbase. Just a week ago, a young woman his sister's age had dropped by with a basket of muffins to thank everyone—Ronan in particular—for rescuing her cat from a high tree limb.

But there was something about that beautiful, brunette waitress. He couldn't stop thinking about her. That didn't happen often. Before the night was over, he would show her he was one of the good guys. Better than just another guy with a bad pickup line.

CHAPTER FOUR

"A *Slippery Nipple* for you." Alison set the glass on the table before the blushing bride-to-be. "And a *Screaming Orgasm* for your mother." She set the second drink in front of the older woman seated to the bride's left.

The table of bachelorettes laughed, the mother of the bride clearly having the best time of all the girls at the table of ten. They were sweet and fun and, holy hell, they were good tippers. She had to send Roseanne a basket of something to thank her for catching the flu. The night had turned out to be a blessing for her post-holiday empty pocketbook. Baby Emmy would be spoiled. As she should be.

"All right, ladies," Megan's voice reverberated around the room and the bar quieted to near silence. "It's time to meet the sexy boys of your 2019 Rapid Falls Firefighter Charity Calendar."

The women screamed twice as loud this time around, and Alison took a moment to lean against the wall and catch her breath. No one would be ordering drinks for the next ten minutes. Not when there was eye candy to be devoured instead of sugary sweet cocktails with the raunchiest names this side of the Mississippi.

Not to mention, she wanted a real look at the flirty fireman. She hadn't really been offended by his comment. In fact, she'd been flattered, but she could never admit it. Especially not around the rest of the waitresses.

On an average night, Roseanne, Roxy, and Ruby—not triplets, but based on their bleached blonde hair and double D breasts, they could be—cleaned up with as many phone numbers as tips stuffed into their aprons. Alison still had five pounds to lose after giving birth to Emmy, but she received lots of men's phone numbers scribbled on napkins and business cards. She had publicly sworn off men, which meant the girls would be merciless if they found out how much the pickup line had melted her.

"Put your hands together for Mr. January," Megan said over the microphone.

Alison smiled as the crowd roared. A sexy forty-something stud emerged from the office and strutted past the tables and onto the stage in a tight tee and a pair of uniformed pants complete with suspenders. He flexed and laughed as the women screamed.

Mr. February and Mr. March followed, a blond and a redhead. Both buff, both smiling like movie stars. Tonight, at Andie's, they were.

"Hey, have a drink with me," Joey called to Alison. "Take a load off for a few."

Alison hurried behind the bar, took a seat in the soft leather office chair he must have rolled out for her, and kicked off her shoes. "This is the life."

Joey passed her a ginger ale with a few maraschino cherries effervescing at the bottom of the flute. "You should wear loafers. No one's looking at your feet."

Alison's laughter was drowned out by another round of screams and catcalls.

"Can you see from back there? Mr. April is pretty cute."

"Too bad you're married, Joey."

Joey smiled and took a swallow of his beer. "Not for me, Ali. For you. Still swearing off men, huh?"

She nodded and took a second to shut her eyes. Emmy was teething, so some nights, sleep was almost nonexistent. It was funny how a loud bar filled with screaming patrons and clanging glasses seemed quieter than a crying baby in a small apartment.

"I'm paying you double time," Joey said.

She opened her eyes. "Aw, Joey, you don't have to do that. I volunteered to take Roseanne's shift."

"And we appreciate it. Considering you hate New Year's Eve as much as Valentine's Day, it's the least I can do."

"I hate it more than Valentine's Day."

He laughed. "Why? New Year's Eve has champagne."

"One word, Joey. Chocolate."

"Ah."

"Chocolate is February fourteenth's only saving grace," she said.

"Better than sex, huh?"

"It's a very, very close second." Alison shrugged. "And the best I'm going to get, at the moment."

"Well then, we truly appreciate you coming in. I'll even bring you chocolate on your next shift."

"You're my favorite boss." Ali looked up at the stage. "Don't tell Megan."

"My wife knows I'm irresistible."

"Seriously, though. I don't mind being here."

"You're exhausted." He held up his hands in defence. "Not that you look tired."

Alison laughed. "Well, thanks for that, at least. It comes with the mom territory. I'm not complaining. I love her to pieces, but the crying"—she grimaced—"is brutal."

"You know what might help?" he said. "Mr. July."

"I don't need a man." When Joey quirked a brow, Alison stood and looked over the bar. "I don't. But I'll cave. What's special about Mr. July?"

Then she saw him. Soft, sandy blond hair, long and wavy, brushed over cheekbones that rivaled those of a male super-model. Full lips pulled up at the corners as the crowd cheered for his seeming shyness. His eyes were downcast, and it was obvious he wasn't comfortable as a calendar boy. Which was insanity, considering he looked the most like one so far.

"You don't recognize him?" Joey asked from behind her.

"No. Why? Should I?" She couldn't look away as Mr. July rubbed the back of his neck, then quickly slid to the right and halted beside his boisterous co-worker who hadn't stopped laughing at his expense.

"He's the one who offered to fuck you."

Ginger ale shot out of Alison's nose, and she choked as the bubbles burned her throat. Joey patted her back and howled with laughter.

"That was weird." She wheezed once her windpipe cleared.

Mr. July stood on the stage, hands clasped in front of him like a good little boy at church.

Alison picked up a clean bar towel from the stack sitting beside the sink and wiped her face. "That was some pickup line."

Joey smiled. "You would be surprised at what I've heard over the years."

"Ditto. But never that one."

"Busy night." Roxy joined them at the bar and passed her order book to Joey.

"And this is the just the beginning," Alison agreed.

Joey started filling Roxy's orders. "I think Mr. July likes you, Ali."

"What?" She blinked. "How can you tell?"

Joey grabbed a beer glass from the mini cooler and began filling it at the tap. "He looked really bummed when he struck out."

Alison shrugged. "I doubt it happens a lot."

Joey set the beer on Roxy's tray alongside two other drinks he'd made.

Roxy lifted her full tray. "I want details later." She disappeared back into the crowd.

Joey took the bar towel from Ali and dabbed at the corner of her mouth. "You're drooling."

Ali rolled her eyes. "I'm going to go fix my lipstick, then get back to work." She winked at Joey. "Earn that double time."

He waggled his brows. "And maybe talk to Mr. July?"

She shook her head. That ship had sailed. No man wanted to get mixed up with a divorcee whose nights were filled with diapers. It didn't help that the baby wasn't her ex-husband's, but the result of a one-night stand with a married man.

Alison was happy with life. Just her and Emmy. Their dreams and all their shoes. There wasn't room in the closet for turnout gear. A mental picture rose of Mr. July *out* of his turnout gear. Those pectorals would feel hard under her hands.

Alison turned and froze

Hell, he was looking right at her.

CHAPTER FIVE

By nine o'clock, the women at Andie's were already giddy. Alison couldn't blame them. All but two of the calendar guys were shirtless. Megan had opened a photo booth with the same photographer who had shot the calendar photographs, and there was a heck of a lot of flirting going on. Autographs seemed popular, too. An excuse to get up close and personal with the guys.

Ruby emerged from her break in the office and crossed to Alison at the bar. "Your turn to sit, gorgeous. Ten minutes and then we need you."

Alison smiled. "Thanks, girl. Ten is all I need."

Alison slipped into the office and kicked off her shoes. Living and working in heels had never been a problem. She loved them. But ever since Emmy's birth, her ankles swelled after she stood too long. Kind of a bad deal considering she made her money on her feet.

She rubbed her sore arches and swung her feet up on Meg's desk. Alison glanced at her new college books, sitting on a nearby chair, still wrapped up tight in plastic. Instead of tearing open the plastic wrap, she grabbed her tattered copy of *Pirate's*

Booty and delved back into the love scene on page ninety-two. Bronze Beard was ravishing a lovely island woman and had all the right moves. The rest of the staff at Andie's teased her mercilessly, but she didn't care. This book was her love life. My God, it was phenomenal.

"Okay, Bronzy. You have three minutes and then I need to start on my reading list. What are you going to do to me tonight?"

She started at the knock on the office door behind her, yanked her feet off the desk and spun in her seat. Mr. July stood in the doorway, one shoulder leaning against the door jamb.

"Sorry. Damn," he said. "I'm not coming off as very smooth tonight. Who's Bronzy?"

Alison tugged her short skirt down to sit like a proper lady.

Mr. July gave her another hundred-watt smile. "Mind if I...?"

He crossed to the desk and sat one hip on the edge. Thank God, the desk was sturdy. The man was huge. Not just muscular, but his presence, his warmth, his smile filled the small office.

"Hi," he said.

The dimples blanked her mind. Normally, she had intelligent things to say. She even knew how to flirt. Well, not really, but staring was weak. Even for her.

"My name is Ronan McGuire," he said. "Mr. July. I would like to apologize for the horrible pickup line out there earlier. It was incredibly rude."

Damn, those dimples. They were so deep.

"So, you don't want to fuck me?"

A faint blush colored his cheeks. She couldn't believe it. The man wasn't just gorgeous, he was sweet as honey.

"What?" he said. "I, well, I..."

Alison laughed. "Now we're even."

He visibly relaxed and extended his hand to shake. "Start over?"

"That's a little cliché."

He shrugged, hand still outstretched. "You're a hard woman to talk to."

"I'm teasing, again."

She grasped his hand and shook, nearly hummed out loud at the warmth of his hand against hers. Her pulsed jumped at the tender way he caressed her thumb with his. The handshake was by far the sexiest on the planet.

She withdrew her hand and cleared her throat. "My name is Alison Walker, but everyone calls me Ali."

"Beautiful," he murmured.

She fought the warmth creeping up her cheeks. "Thank you."

"It's true—and that's not a line."

His full lips were made for a woman's touch. She wanted to trace her fingers over those dimples. To kiss them. Damn, it would be best if she told him she wasn't available. But she didn't want him to leave. What would be the harm in a little conversation?

"Shouldn't you be out there mingling?" Alison asked.

"There's eleven of my brothers out there. No one will miss me."

"Oh, I'm sure they will. You're very handsome."

Ronan dropped his head, but she glimpsed the smile he was clearly trying to hide.

He tilted his head to meet her gaze. "I'm forgiven, then?"

Alison couldn't help but laugh. "Don't worry about it. Joey teases me all the time."

"Joey?"

"The bartender."

"Ah." Ronan nodded.

"He's married to my boss, the beautiful redhead."

"We've met." Ronan regarded her. "So, you're single?"

"I'm unavailable."

His brow furrowed. "Dating?"

"No."

Ronan shook his head. His long hair tussled around his face in way too sexy for words. "What am I missing?"

For a split second, she considered forgetting her oath to swear off men. No, as tempting and alluring and damn delicious as Ronan was, how did she tell him her heart couldn't do one nighters? That was how she ended up with Emmy.

Her sweet baby girl wouldn't know her father because Alison had grown tired of being alone and had spent a hot, sweaty night with a man who put on a great show, who said all the right things, but turned out to be an asshole. Her daughter deserved more.

"Ali?" Ronan asked.

She shook her head. "Sorry, I'm just not...available."

Alison slipped on her shoes, then stood. Ronan rose. He smelled wonderful. Like cinnamon and soap. She lifted her eyes to find him watching her. Her heart began to pound. He had an inviting mouth that would devour her. An unexpected desire bubbled to the surface to throw her arms around his neck and kiss him.

She backed up a step. "I need to get back to work."

His warm hazel eyes remained locked with hers. "Yeah."

He placed warm hands on her hips.

Her cheeks heated. "Ronan." The word came out a plea.

"Still a no?"

Eyes still locked with his, she nodded. "Still a no."

He stepped back and Alison immediately regretted the loss of his heat.

"We still have a few hours until midnight," he murmured. "I'm not giving up on you, Cinderella."

She mustered the strength of a dozen warriors—and maybe two or three soccer moms—and slipped past him.

At the door, she paused and looked over her shoulder. "I'm far from Cinderella."

CHAPTER SIX

Ronan stood at the steps leading up to the stage. Half the guys were seated at a long table. The crowd's hooting and whistling faded into the back of his mind as he covertly watched Alison deliver drinks to a table of women on the far side of the bar.

Fuck, the woman had kept him on the edge of desire from the moment he'd laid eyes on her. He was damned glad he wore his loose-fitting turnout pants. Otherwise, his hardened cock would be putting on a show for the voracious crowd—and he would be scaring the hell out of Alison.

Despite his crappy first impression, she clearly found him attractive. On some primal level, they clicked. Some asshole had undoubtedly broken her heart, though. God, he hated careless men. Ronan liked to think of himself as one of the good guys. Raised by his grandmother and protector to a beautiful sister. He grinned. Good guys gave a woman a reason to trust them. Alison needed to know he wasn't chasing her for a one-night stand. He'd had his fill of one-night stands.

Alison had teased him in the office—a little, at least. He grinned with the memory of her blush when he'd placed his hands on her slim hips. Yeah, she liked him. Maybe the new year wouldn't be so lonely—for either of them.

"There's a lineup of hot chicks waiting for Mr. July." Keith nodded toward the stage. "Move it."

Ronan obliged. Keith followed close behind then pushed him toward the chair beside Mike.

Ronan nodded toward the bar. "Get me a beer, huh, lieutenant?"

"Oh, like this is the hardest work you've ever had to do," Mike said. "Just ask them their names and they'll lean in nice and close to whisper it to you."

"Giving me a full view of the goods, right?" Ronan said.

Mike laughed. "I think you're worse than me."

"Not possible, Mikey."

"Hi," a low, feminine voice said.

Ronan looked up at a beautiful pair of full breasts spilling out of a tight black dress, and then lifted his eyes higher to an equally lovely face. He smiled. "Hi."

The woman set her calendar on the table in front of him, the page open to his photo. "Can you make it out to Sarah?"

Ronan wrote 'To Sarah,' then scribbled his signature over the photo of himself. "Thanks for coming out, tonight."

Sarah smiled and kind of shimmied her dress down, further emphasizing her ample cleavage. She looked at him through her lashes.

"Hey, gorgeous," Mike said.

Sarah's gaze shifted to Mike and her eyes lit. She slid her calendar over to him and Mike gave Ronan a covert wink. Ronan breathed a sigh of relief. He would have to buy Mike a beer later.

"What's your name?" Ronan asked without looking up as a calendar slide before him.

"Kelly Ann McGuire."

Ronan snapped his head up and came face to face with his little sister. Only she didn't look so little. Her floral dress was too short and way, way too damn tight.

"Kel? What are you doing here? In *that*?"

She was only eighteen. Practically a kid.

"Girls' night." She lifted a small digital camera and pointed it at him. A blinding flash followed.

He blinked the spots away from his eyes. "Dammit, no pictures, Kel."

Kelly Ann laughed. "You bought me this camera for Christmas. I have to use it."

He also bought her a gift card for the mall, which she likely used to buy that scrap of fabric she called a dress.

"Doesn't she look amazing?" Her best friend Cara stepped up beside Kelly Ann in an even tighter and shorter dress.

Ronan frowned. "Does Grandma know you're here? It's a bar. You're underage."

When Kelly Ann smiled, he could almost see her with braces, big pink glasses, messy pigtails, and that ratty teddy bear she used to carry under one arm. When did she grow up?

"Of course. I borrowed her car."

He pinned her with a hard stare. "Does she know you're at a bar?"

His sister blew out an exasperated breath. "Ronan."

He shook his head. "Sorry."

Kelly Ann held out her hand to show the big black X marked on her skin. "No drinking. Don't worry. I couldn't even if I tried. They checked everyone's ID at the door."

"Sign our calendars?" Cara asked.

He rubbed the back of his neck, then scribbled his name on the glossy photo of his shirtless body, a flathead axe slung over his shoulder. "I'm just surprised to see you here, Kel, that's all."

"We came for moral support. I know you don't like crowds."

Cara laughed. "Yeah, right. Moral support. We came for the hot men." She flipped the page of her calendar and slid over to Mike. "Hello, handsome. I'm Cara."

"Hi, Cara." God, even Mike's voice sounded dirty.

"Knock it off," Ronan growled. "She's my baby sister's friend."

"Ronan," Cara crossed her arms over her chest, pushing her breasts higher.

Cara had grown up in their house. The girls were sisters without the DNA to match and had been joined at the hip since they were seven. Nothing had changed now that they were in college—which made Cara like another sister to him, so to see her dressed like a sex kitten threw him off his game almost as much as seeing Kelly Ann looking like a grown woman.

He frowned at Cara, who smirked. She knew exactly what she was doing. When she leaned over to whisper something to Mike, Ronan knew she was trouble. If this was what the two of them did when he wasn't around...

Kelly Ann leaned in and kissed his cheek. "I'm an adult, Ronan. You'd better get back to work. Don't worry, it's like ninety percent women here." She stepped over to Mike and the next woman in line laid her calendar in front of Ronan.

"Hi, I'm Tiana," the girl said.

He watched Kelly Ann laugh at something Mike said.

"Dammit, Shepard." Ronan shoved to his feet. His chair slid back hard. It rocked on its legs but didn't fall.

"Ronan, relax," Kelly Ann said.

His sister knew better than to tell him to relax. She was his responsibility. Their grandma had adopted the two of them after their parents died, but he considered himself an equal parent to his sister—which meant making sure she knew what she was getting into with men.

He winced at the memory of the one and only time he'd

tried to teach her exactly what went on between men and women. It was the summer after graduation. He had just snuck Susie Pikeman out of his bedroom window when Kelly Ann opened his bedroom door and walked inside.

"Kel, you have to knock first."

Thank fuck she hadn't come in the room fifteen minutes earlier. At twelve, she had begun to turn from cute to pretty, and she was all kinds of nosey.

"What are you doing up? It's past midnight."

"You and Suzie were loud." She picked up the box of condoms lying on the bed. "What are these?"

Ronan had known this day would come, but to be practically caught in the act and to have to explain... "When two people love each other, sometimes they express their feelings in a physical way."

"Like a hug?"

"Yeah, yeah. Except they hug without clothes on."

"Gross!"

Ronan laughed at her wrinkled-up nose. She was still a kid—despite the fact Grandma had bought her bras last week.

He grabbed a condom and opened it. "Guys put this on their penis to protect the woman they're, um, hugging, from getting pregnant."

"Hugging?"

"Shit, let me try again. When you're older, like at least thirty, you might like a guy and want to kiss him. Anyway, sex is a way two people express their feelings for each other. The man puts his penis into the woman's..." Ronan rubbed the back of his neck and Kelly Ann laughed.

"Relax. Our gym teacher already told us about this."

He blinked. "What? When?"

She shrugged. "Months ago. You have a lot of friends over. Girls. Do you love them all?"

That had been a real wake up call. He didn't take women out or buy them flowers. He just fucked away his grief and loneliness. That wasn't the way he wanted a guy to treat his baby sister—which meant he had to change his ways.

"I can come back?" The poor girl in front of him with her calendar outstretched looked deflated.

"No, no. I'm sorry." Ronan smiled. "Hi, Tiana, right? Thanks for coming out." He tried to concentrate on signing his name, but he could hear Kelly Ann laugh her way from August to December.

"Is everything okay?" Tiana asked.

Ronan flashed another smile. "Absolutely. You know what? Make sure to grab me later and I'll buy you a beer, okay? My treat."

Tiana beamed. "Okay, sure. I'd love that."

He blew out a breath. Damn. First it was Alison. Now his sister. Women would be the death of him.

"Mindi." A busty fifty-something blonde winked and set her calendar on the table in front of him.

Ronan grinned. "With an I or a Y?"

"Any way you like it sweetheart," she purred.

A quick glance behind Mindi told him he had at least another fifty more calendars to sign.

He signed Mindi's calendar and the next woman slid over in front of him.

"Angel," she said.

Ronan couldn't help but smile. The woman in a devil's red dress with hair to match was anything but angelic. "Thanks for coming tonight, Angel."

"Thank *you*. So, is this your night off?"

He nodded. "We just finished our shift this morning. Off for a couple days now."

Ronan caught the glimmer that appeared in her eyes. He

groaned inwardly. Shit. He'd practically thrown her an invitation.

"Oh, yeah? Come home with me tonight, and I'll make you breakfast in the morning."

Mike kicked his boot under the table. "Thanks for the offer, honey, but I have plans." Plans to kiss a beautiful brunette at midnight.

"Can't blame a girl for trying."

Ronan smiled and winked. "No, I can't. But you know who loves breakfast? My buddy." He cuffed Mike on the shoulder.

Angel met his eyes, bit her full bottom lip, then stepped over to Mike.

"Hey, darlin'," Mike said, as Ronan turned his attention to the next woman.

Ronan blinked. The woman who taught him all he knew about chili seasoning, breading pork chops, and whisking the fluffiest meringue stood in front on him in a body-hugging little black number that drew attention to a killer body Ronan hadn't noticed beneath her chef's whites.

He grinned. "Hey, Chef."

Chef Rodrigues was funny, kind, and in Ronan's case, very patient, considering he couldn't crack an egg at the start of his studies. They hadn't hit it off as more than friends. She treated him like any other student and didn't hit on him. It was a nice reprieve from nights out at the bars. A place where he could focus on something besides work.

Seeing Lila as something other than a teacher, well, damn, it threw him off. It was almost like seeing your mom in a bathing suit. He rubbed his neck, hoping he didn't look as embarrassed as he felt. At least, he still had a damn shirt on.

"I didn't take you for a fire groupie," Ronan said, then mentally berated himself for what he had just implied.

Thankfully, she laughed. "Oh, I'm not. My sister dragged me here. Her son spent some time at the Children's Hospital."

Ronan cringed. "Jesus, I'm sorry. How is your nephew?"

Lila smiled and reached across the table to squeeze his shoulder. "Relax. Jeffrey is heathy as a horse. You're usually more pulled together, Ronan."

"Yeah. Sorry. It's been a long night."

She looked at her watch. "Didn't the night just begin?"

He snorted. "Don't remind me."

She laughed and he signed her calendar. "Just have fun with it, Ronan. And thank you. This money means a lot to a lot of people."

He looked up and saw the genuine gratitude in her eyes. That was what this night was all about: the kids who would benefit from the money they raised. The kids... and his sexy Alison. The woman who was so damn far from being his. But if he had it his way...

Speak of the delicious devil. He caught a glimpse of dark chocolate hair, a sexy ass in a body-hugging black dress, and sparkly purple heels strut in front of the stage.

Alison. Dammit.

"Have a good night, Ronan," Lila said. "I'll see you next semester for steaks."

Ronan returned his attention to Lila. "Looking forward to it." He passed her the signed calendar.

Ronan released a breath before smiling at the next pretty girl in line. He had just under three hours to convince Alison to kiss him at midnight. If he was lucky, she would kiss him well into the new year, as well.

CHAPTER SEVEN

FINALLY, MEGAN RETURNED TO THE STAGE, A BROOM IN hand, and Ronan gratefully filed down the stage steps behind his coworkers, who reached the main floor and clustered to the right of the steps.

On stage, Megan called, "Who's ready for a little fun?"

Ronan flexed his hand. Signing autographs was no joke. God, the crowd was insane. He chuckled. Standing in front of fires so hot that he could feel the heat through all the protective gear was easier than facing a room full of lusty women.

Angel sauntered past and looked up at him through her lashes. Ronan blew out a silent whistle. It would be so easy to go home with her. But easy had become mundane.

A soft hand caressed his bicep. "You're thinking too hard."

Ronan recognized Alison's voice and his cock tightened at the warmth of her hand on his skin.

"You're going to give these women the wrong impression."

He turned and faced her. She stood, one hip pushed out to the side, six empty beer glasses balanced on the tray in her hand.

"What impression is that?" he asked.

She tapped her temple. "That you think with your upstairs brain."

He snorted. "Is that bad?"

Alison's deep green eyes locked with his. "In a room full of women who want the other head, it is."

"But not you?"

"Not me."

"You like this head?" Ronan tapped his temple.

"You have an attractive face." She smiled. "Think about that, pretty boy."

She turned and headed back to the bar. Ronan watched the sway of her hips and knew, at the moment, he wasn't thinking with his upstairs brain. Alison had his attention. Not just for one night. He wanted to get to know her.

Well, damn. He was thinking with his upstairs brain, after all. Ronan grinned. She would like that. *Maybe.*

"Mr. July? Are you going to volunteer in our first game?" Megan's voice boomed over the microphone.

Mike pushed him toward the stairs before he knew which game he agreed to. He glared at Mike then climbed the stairs and crossed to where Megan stood.

"What am I getting myself into?" Ronan whispered.

Megan grasped his arm and pulled him in front of the microphone. "Easy stuff. I promise." She pointed at Ronan and the crowd went wild. She lifted on tiptoes to bring her mouth close to the microphone and said, "So, ladies, Mr. July is hot, don't you agree?"

Female screams mingled with loud laughter from the firemen at the big table near the stage. Ronan shook his head. Next year, he would just make a sizable donation to the children's hospital.

"So, why is he still wearing a shirt?" Megan said into the microphone.

"You want me to strip?" Ronan started when his whispered words filled the room. He snapped his eyes onto the microphone, then back onto the crowd when a woman in the back of the room shouted, "Take it off!"

Ronan hesitated, then caught sight of Alison behind the bar —watching. Slowly, he slid his suspenders off his shoulders to the roar of screams.

"Wait, wait, wait. Ladies?" Megan pulled the microphone from its stand. "Do you think he needs some help taking that shirt off?"

Ronan shot a look at Megan, and she bit her lip before mouthing, "Please."

He looked back at Alison. Oh, this could get interesting.

Ronan wrapped his hand around Megan's and pulled the microphone to his lips. "Well, Megan. I'll agree to this. But only if I can choose the volunteer."

Hands shot up throughout the bar.

"All right," Megan said. "Who's the lucky lady?"

Ronan pointed into the crowd and moved his arm back and forth, eliciting more cheers. Hey, a guy could get into this. He stopped his finger on Alison. "The lovely lady behind the bar. Come on up."

Alison's mouth dropped open. Her mouth closed, and the look of shock turned into a narrow-eyed I'll-get-you-for-this look.

Oh, this was going to be good.

Ronan kept his eyes locked with hers and crooked his finger in a come-on-up motion. She shook her head. He laughed when the bartender grasped her shoulders and eased her around the bar. She whirled and swatted his hands away, then spun toward the stage. Back straight, Alison strutted across the room in her sky-high heels and then up the stairs onto the stage.

"I'm going to kill you," she said through her teeth.

"Oh, a romantic, huh?" he whispered.

He wrapped his arms around her in a hug. She let her arms hang down at her sides. At least she smiled, despite the blush.

"Okay, Ali," Megan said as Ronan drew back, "show us what this Calendar Boy has under that uniform."

Alison could have yanked the shirt over his head and strutted off stage. But not Alison. On stage, in front of a couple hundred women, she seemed to want him. He had sensed her interest in the bar's office, too.

At least eight inches shorter than him—despite those crazy high heels—Alison smiled up at him, her lush hair framing her face. "Let's do this, hero."

She struck him speechless as she flattened her palms against his abs. Through the thin fabric of his shirt, her nails dug into his flesh with enough pressure to make his throat go dry. He swallowed, thankful again he wore turnout pants, as his cock hardened into a serious erection.

Her lips quirked up at the corners. A little dimple appeared high on her left cheek, right before she yanked his shirt up to reveal his chest and stomach. The shocked expression on her face when she came face-to-pecs with his pierced nipples made him want to beg her to give the rings a tug. When she licked her lips, he thought he would come in his boxer briefs.

Losing a bet to Mike over a game of pool had seemed like a shitty deal at the time, and getting his nipples pierced had hurt like hell—far worse than the tattoo on his shoulder—but women loved the nipple rings. Including Alison, obviously.

He grinned. "Like those?"

She could deny it all she wanted, but desire was written all over her face. Written with a blush so deep, he could only guess how much more turned on she would be when she saw the other piercing on his body. *If* he earned the chance to show it to her.

Without a word, she pushed his shirt up to his shoulders,

careful to avoid his nipples. He wasn't sure which of them was more tortured by her evasion.

"Let me help you out." Ronan crossed his arms and pulled his shirt over his head.

A mental image flashed of her in his house wearing nothing but his t-shirt.

Ronan handed her the shirt. "Here you go, little lady."

Alison smiled, brought the balled-up shirt to her nose, and sniffed. "Mm."

Ronan stared. The woman would kill him before night's end.

The ladies in the crowd screamed, and Alison twirled the shirt over her head and tossed it into the horny mob. Ronan laughed. Where had these girls been during high school?

"Great work, Ali." Megan said, her voice loud in the microphone. "What do you think, ladies? Better shirtless?"

"Take your pants off," someone yelled.

Alison turned back to Ronan and patted his abs. "You owe me for this."

He owed her? Ronan flexed his pecs, making his nipple rings jump a little. "Let me know when you want a favor, honey." He winked, then pulled his suspenders back up over his shoulders.

She snorted and shook those damn sexy hips as she walked off stage.

By the end of the night, after his kiss—which was going to set off every smoke detector in the building—Ronan would get her phone number.

CHAPTER EIGHT

ALISON HAD TABLES TO CHECK, DRINKS TO REFILL, BUT SHE couldn't stop watching the action on stage. More specifically, she couldn't take her eyes off a now shirtless Ronan.

"Is that my whole punishment?" Ronan crossed his arms over his chest.

"Oh, no, sweetheart. We're just getting started." Megan's devious grin held in place as she faced the crowd. "The name of the game is to see how well these firemen can handle their, well, how should I say it, their poles." Megan held up the broom she gripped in her left hand.

Alison laughed when Megan slid the broom between Ronan's legs, so that the broomstick stuck out in the front like a very long, very thin erection. Ronan dropped his head back and laughed as the table of firefighters she had delivered beers to hollered and cheered. But Ronan played along like a good sport and shook his broom appendage around to the elation of the crowd.

"That's pretty accurate," said the cute blond fireman sitting nearest to Alison at the table near the stage.

While Alison felt certain the real thing was a lot better than the old broom from the office, she would never look at that broom the same way.

She laughed. "Does Ronan date a lot? With a three-foot penis, I would assume he's pretty popular with the ladies."

The blond laughed. "He does all right. But he's the shy one in the group."

Ronan shook his hips so his broom handle penis bobbed to the cheesy stripper-style music Megan played.

"Shy?" Alison said.

"Generally." The firefighter took a swallow of his beer. "Hey, can I get some wings?"

"BBQ, honey garlic, or hot and spicy?"

"I'm Trevor, by the way."

"Ali. I recommend the BBQ. Sweet and sticky."

Trevor smiled. "Sounds like my kind of night."

"We're still talking about chicken wings, right?" Alison asked as she gathered empty beer glasses from the table.

"We can talk about anything you like."

Alison shook her head with a good-natured smile. "Wings, coming right up." She hurried to the bar to drop off the glasses and place the order.

"You looked pretty hot up there," Joey said. "Looks like your lack of dating experience hasn't affected your ability to strip a man of his clothes."

"Like riding a bike."

Alison turned her back to the bar to check on her tables. Everyone's eyes were glued to the stage. A young girl was bent over at the waist, a roll of toilet paper squeezed between her thighs while Ronan attempted to slide the broom stick into the hole.

The verdict: he was horrible at it.

Nearly doubled over with laughter, Megan could barely speak into the microphone.

Ronan waddled over to her, the broom handle clamped between his thighs, and took the microphone from her. "This does not imply anything, okay?"

"Of course not," Megan managed between giggles.

Ronan turned, and Alison caught sight of a tattoo on his right shoulder. He turned back to the crowd before she could get a close enough look, but it was a crest of some kind, like the fire department logo on his shirt. Her fingers twitched with the desire to trace the tattoo.

A sexy fireman took the stairs to the stage two at time. In three paces, he reached Ronan and grabbed the broom. He pulled his own shirt off and tossed it out at the bachelorette's table.

"Let me show him how it's done," he said to cheers from the crowd.

Ronan laughed.

Warmth rippled through Alison. What was it about him that drew her in so deeply? He was sexy as sin. But on top of that pretty face and incredible body, he was sweet—and he genuinely seemed interested in her.

As a cocktail waitress, Ali was accustomed to flirty men. She was attentive to their needs, even if it was simply pizza and beer—which was more attention than some guys received—so they naturally thought she was flirting. She didn't mind providing the ego boost from time to time. That was not attraction, though. It had only been six months since she had delivered Emmy. Her hips were wider, her curves softer, and she hadn't felt sexy in over a year. She hated to admit it, but Ronan made her feel attractive.

"Let's hear it for Danni," Megan said, as the crown applauded. "And, of course, both Mr. July and Mr. September."

Ronan wrapped his arm around his poor victim and kissed the top of her head. The other fireman had a new volunteer and shoved the phallic broomstick into the toilet paper tube as if he was a sex master. The crowd of women screamed their approval.

Alison grabbed a few more drink orders and returned to the bar for Trevor's wings. "I'm sure you could teach him a thing or two," Joey said.

Alison shot him a narrow-eyed look. "I am not dating him, much less having sex with the man."

He lifted a brow. "He's not Jerimiah."

She started. Tears pricked.

"Shit, I'm sorry," Joey said.

Alison swiped at a tear. "No. It's fine."

He reached across the bar and squeezed her hand that still gripped a beer glass. "Hey, say the word, and he's out of here."

She wanted to cry again but for a different reason. Joey had been through hell overseas with the army. An IED had gone off five feet from where he stood. During the long recovery, never once had he complained. Now he was protecting her.

"You okay, Alison?" his voice cut through her reverie.

She smiled. "Never better."

"Looks good," Trevor said when she set the wings in front of him a minute later. "How about you join me for something sweet and sticky?"

She laughed. "You better be talking about the wings."

He grinned, but she spun and headed back to the bar. What would she have said if Ronan had made the same offer?

CHAPTER NINE

"How is it that I have never seen you shirtless, Ronan?" Cara asked as he neared the table where she and Kelly Ann sat.

The forty-something sleazeball talking to his sister looked over his shoulder at Ronan. When their eyes met, he spun and wound his way through the tables toward the bar.

Ronan returned his attention to the girls and sank into a chair. "You've seen me shirtless, Cara."

"When? I think I would remember"—Cara ran her hand over Ronan's bare shoulder—"all of this."

Ronan grasped her hand and set it back on the table in front of her. "At the beach, when I mowed the lawn. I could go on. Kel–"

"I don't think you were this buff," Cara interrupted. "I mean, you were always toned but damn, Ronan. You're hot."

This wasn't new—her schoolgirl crush, which he always thought was cute—and she wouldn't distract him from a lecture. "Cara. You're like a sister to me. You know that."

Cara went on as if she hadn't heard, "And the nipple rings. I can appreciate–"

Ronan covered her mouth with his hand. "I'm calling you a cab."

Kelly Ann sighed. "Stop acting like a grandpa. We're having fun."

"But that guy, Kel–"

"He's just being friendly. Please let us stay." Kelly Ann batted her eyelashes and smiled, knowing he would give her anything she asked. Always had, always would.

He sighed. "Just until midnight, and then I'm calling you a cab."

"I have Granny's car."

"Okay. I'll walk you to the parking lot. I don't care what I'm doing, get me. I mean it."

Cara pushed Ronan's hand off her mouth. "Did you smudge my lipstick?" She turned to Kelly Ann. "He did. Didn't he?"

Without another word, Cara stood and pulled Kelly Ann toward the bathrooms.

Damn, those were short dresses.

"A little young for you? Or is that your thing?"

Ronan turned as Alison set her tray on the girls' table.

"That was my baby sister and her bad influence of a best friend."

She smiled, and he realized she was relieved.

Alison set an empty glass on the tray. "Moral support?"

"She's here to gather blackmail, I'm sure."

Alison laughed. "I hope she's taking photos. Lots of them. This is material to show your grandchildren someday."

Ronan smiled. "You think so, huh?"

Her head snapped up. When her cheeks pinked, he knew he had her.

He stood and stepped closer. "What kind of pictures should they take?"

She stared up at him for three heartbeats, then dropped her

gaze and began wiping down the table. "That might be strange. *Look how ripped Grandpa was*," she said in a lisping baby voice. "Though the broomstick penis does need to be preserved for posterity."

Before he could come up with a smart remark, she scooped up the tray and headed back to the bar.

"So, is Cara dating anyone?"

Ronan turned to face Mike. "She's eighteen."

"And?"

Ronan crossed his arms. "You want me to kick your ass?"

Mike laughed and punched his shoulder. "I'm just messing with you." He handed Ronan one of the two beer bottles he held, then clinked his bottle against Ronan's and took a swig. "There's a group of horny women who have requested a picture with us in the photo booth. Come on, Dad."

Ronan followed Mike to the corner of the bar where the photographer smiled at a group of girls standing beside her. He shot a smile at the girl with a bright-red face. It was damn cute. She looked so nervous.

"Having fun?" he asked her, his hand gentle on her lower back.

She giggled and nodded as if he were Brad Pitt. "It's my birthday."

"Ah. Well, we had better make it memorable, huh?" He swung her into his arms, bridal style. Her friends laughed and cheered as Ronan carried her to the tacky red tinselled wall and turned around for the photograph.

"Say burnin' love," the photographer said before snapping the photo.

Ronan set the birthday girl down and wrapped his arms around her shoulders. "Happy Birthday, honey."

"Thank you." She looked up at him with wide eyes and trembled in his arms.

"Anytime." He gave her a quick peck on the cheek.

The rest of the girls walked into the photo booth all wearing plastic helmets, with Mike, Rogers, and Peters trailing behind. He caught sight of Alison watching from the bar.

He looked at his watch. Ten o'clock. Two hours left to convince her to kiss him at midnight.

CHAPTER TEN

ALISON ENTERED MEGAN'S OFFICE, LIFTED THE PHONE receiver to her ear, and twirled the retro phone cord around her fingers. "Hi, Mom."

"Sorry to interrupt you at work, but Emmy's having a rough night," her mom replied. "Nothing I'm doing is helping put her to sleep. Dad drove her around the block a few times, and I tried a warm bath."

"Did you feed her? Sometimes a warm bottle helps settle her," Alison said.

"No luck."

Alison massaged her lower back. "Put the phone on speaker, Mom. I'll sing to her. That usually helps."

She heard her mom whispering to Emmy. The sweetness in her mom's voice broke her heart. Alison wished so much she could be there with her daughter when she needed her.

"She's listening. Emmy, it's Mommy."

"Hi, sweetie," Alison said. "Are your teeth hurting you, baby?"

Emmy cooed and whined into the phone.

Alison closed her eyes and began singing, *"The itsy-bitsy*

spider climbed up the waterspout. Down came the rain and washed the spider out. Out came the sun and"—the floor creaked behind her, and she spun to find Ronan leaning against the door frame with his arms crossed over his chest—*"dried up all the rain."* She narrowed her eyes. *"And the itsy-bitsy spider climbed up the spout again."*

Ronan's playful smile lit his face and revealed his dimples.

Alison cringed inwardly. How much of her off-key rendition of "Itsy-Bitsy Spider" had he heard?

"She's stopped crying," her mom said. "Thanks, Alison."

Alison sighed and a little of the tension slipped from her shoulders. "Of course, Mom. Thanks again. For everything. I'll see you tomorrow morning."

"We love you," her mom said. "Happy New Year."

"Same to you. Give Dad a hug. Goodnight."

Ronan applauded as Alison hung up the phone. "Boy or girl?"

She frowned. "What?"

"Is your baby a boy or girl?"

Her pulse skipped a beat. "You know?"

"I would have to be pretty dense not to get that you were singing to a baby." He shrugged. "Moms usually sing to their babies. Well?"

"Well, what?"

"A boy or girl."

"Oh." Embarrassment warmed her cheeks. "A girl. Emmy. She's beautiful."

"Not surprising. Her mother is a knockout."

Alison narrowed her eyes again. "Laying it on a little thick, don't you think, Mr. July?"

"Not even close, Alison."

His gaze bore into her, and it took all her nerve not to look away. She squared her shoulders. "It's okay if you don't stay."

Ronan's brow furrowed. "What do you mean?"

"I have a baby."

His frown deepened, then his expression cleared. "You think I would run as fast as I can the other way because you have a child? Whew, that's a relief."

Her heart took a dive. "What?"

"I thought I scared you off with the whole broomstick routine. Now that I know your only concern is that you have a baby, well"—Ronan's nonchalance was undone by the smile that tugged at his mouth—"babies love me."

Alison laughed. "You're terrible."

He grimaced. "Do me a favor."

She stopped laughing. "What?"

"Never tell Emmy that the night we met, I did that routine."

Alison swallowed. Did he really believe he'd be around when Emmy was old enough to hear the story? Her heart beat faster. She forced a look she hoped mirrored his own mock seriousness and said, "We'll see. It's quite a story."

She couldn't help a smile at the memory of this hunk of a man awkwardly gyrating on the stage. There was no way she would ever forget that image. "Really. I blame Megan for that."

"Me, too." He stepped closer, making the office seem too small, too warm. He lifted a hand as if to touch her face, then seemed to catch himself and folded his hands in front of him. "Listen. I know I must seem borderline pathetic following you around like a lost puppy, but –"

"Borderline?"

He laughed. "Touché."

She smiled. "I'm only teasing."

"You're good at it. I can never tell."

"You make me nervous," she blurted.

His eyebrows shot up and she inwardly grimaced. She had to get a grip.

He stepped back. "I'm sorry. Do you want me to go?"

"Oh, no. I mean—it's not a bad thing. It's just been so long."

His returning smile made her breath catch.

"It's the dimples," she breathed.

"I shouldn't smile?" He contorted his face into an approximation of soap opera woe.

She laughed. "No. Please smile. It would be a disservice to the rest of the world if you stopped."

He studied her for a moment. "I like you, Alison."

"Thank you."

He frowned.

"What?" she asked.

Warmth rippled through her when he was so intently focused on her.

"I hoped for, 'I like you, too,'" he said.

"Oh." Butterflies skittered across the inside of her stomach. "Well, I like you, too."

"Are you saying that to humor me, or do you really mean it?"

"I mean it."

He stepped closer, and her eyes were mere inches from his chest. Alison reached up and ran the pad of her thumb in a circle around his nipple.

"Jesus." He groaned. Exactly like he would sound in the bedroom, she was sure.

That groan might be the most erotic sound she had ever heard.

"Did these hurt?" She tucked her pinky finger inside the gold ring that pierced his left nipple and gave it a gentle tug.

"To be honest, I don't know. I can't think straight right now." His voice was raspy, like a man in the desert without water. "When you touch me like that, I can't even remember my birthday."

She hazarded a glance at his face. He stared; eyes locked on her lips.

Her heart jumped into overdrive.

Alison released the ring and backed up a step. "I need to get back to work."

"Alison. Wait."

"I'm sorry. I can't."

She turned and hurried from the room.

CHAPTER ELEVEN

"You can't what?" Ronan caught up with Alison as she emerged from the hallway into the bar. He grasped her hand. "Wait a minute, Alison."

She shook her head. "I have to get back to work. Maybe a cocktail waitress isn't as glamorous a profession as a fireman, but it's my job."

Ronan's chest constricted. She appeared to be on the verge of tears.

Alison tugged, and he released her hand. She hurried to a table of women with near-empty glasses. He walked over to the bar and took a seat on a stool. So, she was a mother. That was unexpected. But, to his surprise, the idea appealed to him. He'd always been a family man, and kids were definitely in his future.

She wasn't out for a one-night stand. She couldn't be. She had her daughter to consider. Ronan's job now was to prove to her he wasn't like the other men she usually dealt with at the bar.

"She's a fiery one."

Ronan looked up at the bartender, who pushed a shot glass

filled with an amber liquid toward him. Ronan tossed back the shot. The bourbon slid down his throat like velvet.

"Thanks, man. I needed that."

"No problem," Joey replied.

"Look, I distracted Alison back there. She didn't take an extra break. I take the blame completely."

The crowd roared, and they both looked at the stage. A girl in a short skirt had just taken a shot off Mike's abs.

"You've knocked her off her game," Joey said.

Ronan returned his attention to the bartender. "I don't follow."

"She hasn't dated since she got pregnant." The bartender wiped down the counter. "I think you could be good for her."

"Yeah?"

"Oh, yeah. You seem like a decent guy, not just out here for a good time like your buddy onstage there."

Ronan nodded slowly. "Unfortunately, I don't think she agrees with you."

Alison stepped up to the bar on Ronan's right. "Two beers, Joey."

Ronan angled his head so he could make eye contact with Alison. She was flat out stunning. Eyes sparkling with life, full lips begging to be kissed. He knew he was a goner when he decided even her nose was cute.

She met his eyes, then looked away too quickly.

"I think you're a great waitress," he said.

She snorted at Ronan's lame apology, then picked up her loaded tray and headed back into the crowd.

Ronan blew out a breath. "She's humoring me. Once tonight is over, she won't want anything to do with me."

Joey wiped down the bar. "Did you insult her job? Because we couldn't run this place without her."

Ronan shook his head. "I tried to kiss her."

Joey laughed. "That'll do it. She's looking for reasons not to like you."

Ronan gave a slow nod. "She's scared."

"Love is a scary thing, man," Joey said, then turned and nodded at another waitress. "What do you need, Ruby?"

Ronan wouldn't know about love. Not really. He had never really cared enough about a woman to fear losing her. Alison intrigued him. She was as unpredictable as fire. Just when you thought you had it under control, there could be a flare up. A flash.

"Can Alison take a five-minute break?" Ronan asked Joey.

"She can have ten, if that's all you need."

"Thanks, man."

Before he lost his nerve, Ronan walked across the room.

A sweet, young girl Kelly Ann's age touched his arm. "Excuse me. I'm missing your autograph." She extended her calendar toward him, open to the page with his picture.

"Well, we can't have that, can we?" Ronan pulled the felt tip marker out of the side pocket in his turnout pants and signed his name over his photo. "What's your name, sweetheart?"

"Beth."

"Beautiful Beth." He handed her the calendar, then kissed her cheek. "Thanks so much for supporting the Rapid Falls Children's Hospital."

Her cheeks pinked. "Oh, um. Of course."

Ronan turned to see where his sexy waitress had disappeared, then turned and caught sight of her back at the bar talking to Joey. Joey was laughing, but she looked pissed.

Ronan crossed the room, not making eye contact with anyone in case he was distracted once more. He stopped inches behind Alison. Her floral perfume wafted up to him.

"May I borrow you for a moment?" he asked.

She twisted and looked at him over her shoulder. "I have to take these drinks to that table over there." She pointed at a nearby table to his left.

Ronan picked up the tray and headed over to the table she had indicated. "Ladies," he said, once he reached the table.

A middle-aged woman rubbed her hand down his bare back and squeezed his ass. "Service with a smile."

Ronan tried not to cringe. This must be what it was like to be a male stripper.

"I do what I can."

Was this what Alison dealt with on a daily basis? Hopefully without the ass grabs. It had to be exhausting. She was the hero. Not him.

"I had the *Blow Job*," a woman with blue-grey hair said, her voice loud enough to carry over the noise of the crowded room.

"Anyone know which one that is?" he asked.

"The one with the whip on top," a blonde waitress said as she passed him.

"Thanks. And the rest?"

The rest of the women reached across the table, eager to show off cleavage as they grabbed their drinks.

The woman with the shot glass rubbed her hand over his chest. "Thanks, Mr. July."

"Enjoy your drinks." Ronan caught the eye of the brunette across the table. The one with the ginger ale. "Wait a minute. Janis?"

She flushed and laughed. "Busted. You weren't supposed to recognize me."

"You look, uh, well, you look—like a girl."

"Hey." Janis pressed her fingertips to her red cheeks.

Ronan went around the table to her chair. "Why didn't you tell me you were coming tonight?"

"I didn't want you to tease me, McGuire. I thought I could hide in the crowd."

"I'm the one making an ass out of myself." Ronan couldn't believe how shy his otherwise bold friend seemed in the crush of lustful women and sweaty firemen. "A woman as pretty as you could never blend in."

"Don't flirt. I'm married."

"Yeah, yeah. Matty knows me. Anyway. Have a good night. I'll come back over later and sign your calendars."

"Or our cleavage?" asked her friend.

Janis rolled her eyes. "Thanks, Ronan." She narrowed her eyes in mock seriousness. "Not a word of this at work."

"Lips are sealed." He turned to find Alison behind him, arms crossed under her amazing breasts, watching him. Had he taken too long? Had she thought he was flirting with Janis?

"You're good at that," she said.

"Waiting tables?" He shook his head. "Not really. No."

She took his empty tray and started back toward the bar. He hurried to follow.

"You're popular with the customers," she said.

They stopped at the bar, and he flashed a smile. "It's probably because I'm topless."

She snorted. "You're probably right."

"Would you believe I couldn't recognize a blowjob when I saw one?"

Her eyes darted to his crotch, then she met his gaze squarely. "I don't believe it. It must not have been done right."

Thank God she was flirting again.

Alison pushed a lock of her thick hair behind her ear.

He took her hand in his. "You have a five-minute break."

Alison shot a narrow-eyed look at Joey, who shrugged.

"Come take a photo with me," Ronan said.

"No."

Ronan blinked. "What? Why not?"

She looked over her shoulder. "Everyone is watching."

Everyone? Then he realized what she meant. His firefighting brothers.

He shrugged. "You're gorgeous. It's understandable."

She rolled her eyes, and he wanted to kiss her. Hard. Instead, he said, "I want something to remember tonight by."

"That's sweet." She smiled. "But no."

"Consider it an apology for your earlier drama?"

She narrowed her eyes, but he saw the amusement she struggled to hide. "You sure you're not a lawyer?"

"Not smart enough."

"You have an answer for everything. I think you would be a great lawyer."

"You're stalling," he said.

"They're still watching."

Ronan grinned. "Embrace the fear, baby." He crouched down, threw his arms around her hips, and lifted her off her feet.

Alison squeaked and threw her arms around his neck. She was trying not to smile but couldn't seem to help herself. "Are you serious?"

The bar erupted in cheers as he started toward the photo booth to the left of the stage. Alison gasped, and the next thing Ronan knew, she'd wrapped her legs around his waist and buried her head against his neck. Damn, her cheek was so warm against his skin and her breasts felt so right pressed against the hard planes of his chest. He was damn glad for his loose-fitting turnout pants.

"I'm next!" a woman called from one of the tables.

"Go, Ronan," Mike shouted.

"I can walk," Alison said against his skin.

Ronan shook his head. "Nope. You're on break."

"*Ronan.*"

Her breath fanned across his flesh. His balls drew up with desire. He wouldn't be getting any sleep tonight.

"Shoot. There's a line," he said. Sure, it was only two other couples, but a line was a line. "Looks like this is going to take more than five minutes."

Alison lifted her head and let her legs fall from around his waist, obviously assuming he would set her down.

He didn't.

She frowned. "Um..."

Ronan smiled at her, tightened his hold, and enjoyed the press of her ass in his hands. He patted her thigh. "Wrap your legs around me. Make this easier on me."

She brought her face inches from his. "People are staring."

"Like I said, they're only looking because you're a damn knockout."

"I feel like you're trying to make me mad." But as she said the words, she wrapped her legs around his hips.

It was difficult to think straight with her breasts brushing his piercings, but he managed to ask, "How so?"

She shook her head, still fighting a gorgeous smile. "You're impossible."

"When you get to know me, I'm actually quite likeable."

"Who was the woman you were talking to? She's beautiful."

"Beautiful? Who?" He couldn't concentrate with her legs so tight around his waist.

"The woman at the table you delivered drinks to," Alison said.

"Janis?" In his experience, women didn't ask about other women in a man's life unless they were interested in that man.

"I work with her. Sort of. She's Rapid Fall's PD. And don't tell anyone, but she's pregnant."

"Who's the daddy?"

Ronan looked up into Alison's eyes. "Her husband Matt. Good guy. Kind of nerdy." He lifted a brow. "You didn't think I was the daddy?"

Her eyes grew wide as saucers. "No."

"I dated her, though. In high school."

"Oh."

Ronan kind of liked the flare of jealousy in her eyes. Maybe not a flare, but a spark. It was something. It was enough.

He winked at Alison. "She couldn't handle me."

The line moved too fast. The photographer faced them. "Who's up?"

I am, he thought, but said, "We are."

"You can put me down now," Alison said.

"Nope." He grabbed a plastic fireman's helmet from the small prop table and set it on her head.

The photographer brought her camera up to her face. "Smile." The camera flashed, and she laughed. "Awesome. Hey, Ronan. Flex for me."

He levered his right arm more securely under Alison's ass, then flexed his left arm and looked at her. Alison shook her head in mock disapproval, but a corner of her mouth twitched upward in a smile. She was fucking beautiful.

The camera flashed. She frowned, then pushed at his chest. He set her on the floor.

"Five minutes is up." She backed up several paces, turned, and hurried to the bar.

There was that damn wall, again. Ronan took a twenty from his pocket and passed it to Sheila.

"You don't have to pay for it, babe," she said.

"It's for charity."

"Thank you." Sheila tucked the money into her cleavage. "You've resorted to kidnapping the girls, now, huh?"

He turned and watched Alison walking, tray in hand, a smile on her face. He hadn't come on too strong. "The woman is a workaholic. I do what I have to do."

CHAPTER TWELVE

"That man's insane." Alison passed out another round of beers at the firefighters' table. A few women had joined them, but for the most part, they had a monopoly on the two tables closest to the stage.

"Who?" the cutie to her left asked. "McGuire?"

"Yes."

"Because he carried you across the bar?"

She grimaced. "You saw that, huh?"

He had a youthful face and incredible pecs. "I think most people did."

"Which month are you?" she asked.

"October."

Alison smiled. "I like October."

He sat up straighter. "Oh, yeah?"

"Yeah."

"I can see why McGuire likes you," he said.

"Aw, you're sweet. Thanks." Alison smiled and draped her arm around his neck. "So, he's not dating?"

She ignored his glance at her chest. In his defense, she had positioned it in front of his face. She hoped he couldn't hear her heart pound in anticipation of an answer she might not like.

Mr. October shook his head. "No. McGuire's not dating. He rarely dates."

"Too busy controlling who Kelly Ann dates," another fireman said, who she recalled was Mr. January.

Alison gave a cool nod. "That's sweet."

"What's sweet?"

Alison flushed at the rumble of Ronan's voice. Her pulse picked up more speed with the warmth of his hand on her lower back.

She removed her arm from Mr. October's shoulders and faced Ronan.

His eyes twinkled when he said, "Don't listen to them. They lie."

She rubbed her hands up his chest and his muscles flexed under her touch. "You're not sweet?"

Ronan pulled her tight against his side. "I'm whatever you want me to be."

Heat pooled in her belly. "A bit of both, please," Alison said in a breathy voice she didn't recognize.

One corner of his mouth lifted in a hint of a smile and those damn dimples made another appearance. "Done," he murmured.

Her heart began to beat faster. He was incredible. Sexy, built, with a charming personality. The best part, he genuinely seemed to like her.

Guilt crept in.

She flirted one minute and pushed him away the next. It was unfair, but she couldn't seem to help herself. It had been too long since she'd felt wanted, and his arms felt so good. A little time with this handsome man wouldn't kill her.

"Okay, everybody," Megan said into the microphone. Her

voice carried over the Dolly Parton classic booming through the small bar. Joey must have chosen the playlist. "One hour until we ring in the New Year. Let's dance."

The firefighters all smiled. Their grins were contagious. Considering most of the patrons at Andie's were women tonight, the boys wouldn't be hurting for dance partners.

Ronan's lips brushed the shell of her ear. "Dance with me."

All she could think was, *Yes. A million times yes.*

Alison cast a look at the bar. Joey motioned her forward with his chin. She should have resisted but allowed Ronan to lead her onto the dance floor.

With one hand pressed tightly to the small of her back, he pulled her flush with his body and began to sway to Chris Isaac's *Wicked Game*. Oh God, she loved this song and Ronan's hips swayed expertly with the music. Alison kept her eyes level with his chest. She was in trouble.

"What made you change your mind?" he asked.

She made the mistake of looking up at him.

He stared down at her, eyes intent on her face. "Ten minutes ago, I had to carry you to the photo booth, and now—"

She squeezed his shoulders. "I'm dancing with you."

"With no excuses."

She moved her hand to poke him in the side. "My job isn't an excuse."

"I know."

Alison shrugged. "I like you."

His eyes darkened. "You just figured that out?"

She dropped her gaze and whispered, "I don't have a great history with men. Emmy's dad isn't a part of her life."

He hugged her tight. "I'm sorry."

She tilted her head back and looked up at him. "I'm not. He wasn't father material. He wasn't even good sex material."

Ronan's brows shot up. Even his neck was attractive, thick and ropey.

"I don't want to know about his sex material, Alison."

"Oh."

He leaned close, brushed his lips over the shell of her ear and whispered, "I'm glad you're giving me a chance."

He drew back and his gaze met hers, then dropped to her mouth. Oh God, was he going to kiss her? Panic sent her heart into a wild rhythm. She wanted him to kiss her but not here. Not on the dancefloor. Not with the entire fire department and bar watching.

Alison flattened a palm on his chest. Her knees weakened when the steel-like muscles beneath her fingers seemed to tighten, but she forced calm and said, "At midnight."

She broke free of his hold and left him standing in the middle of the dancefloor looking stunned. She forced a slow walk back to the bar. What had she done? There was only an hour until the clock struck midnight. One hour until she had to make good on her promise.

Joey set three margaritas on Ruby's tray as Alison reached the bar. Ruby winked at her as she walked past.

Joey took the three empty tumblers sitting on the counter and set them in the sink. "Good for you."

Alison blew out a breath. "Are you going to take ten minutes off my check?"

He considered or pretended to consider—the amused curve of his mouth gave him away—then said, "Never. I'm a sucker for love."

She rolled her eyes. "Love? That's going a little far, don't you think?"

He passed her a glass full of ginger ale. "I knew Meg was the only woman for me the moment I saw her."

Megan stepped up beside her and wrapped her arm around

Alison. "You looked great out there. I would have pegged you for a Mr. March type, but I definitely approve of your choice. Mr. July is a sweetheart."

Alison hesitated, then said, "I told him I would kiss him at midnight."

Megan blinked, then bit her lip. "Oh, Alison. I have bad news."

Alison tensed.

"Ronan offered to auction off his New Year's Eve kiss." Megan squeezed her hand. "Alison, honey. It's for the kids. It doesn't mean anything. I'm sure he would much rather kiss you."

Alison's cheeks heated with embarrassment. She was a fool. "I'm going to get some supplies from the back."

When she reached the storage room, Alison closed the door behind her and leaned back against the cool metal. Butterflies in her belly danced a tango. The auction was for charity and she admired Ronan for taking part. This money went to the Children's Hospital. Still, she wanted that kiss.

God, she hadn't been this attracted to a man in ages. A man who would start the new year with his full lips pressed against another woman's mouth. Had she been this attracted to Emmy's father Jerimiah?

His British accent had caught her attention. And that he was markedly more sophisticated than the typical Andie's customers. He'd worn a dove gray suit, a white shirt unbuttoned at the collar, and no tie. He drank scotch. Neat.

She still felt embarrassed at how easily she had given in to his proposition. When he took her to a motel—not even a hotel— instead of to his home, she should have heeded the warning bell in her head. But she'd been lonely, and he made her feel pretty after the divorce. They didn't make love. They fucked.

He had tried to sneak out, and she couldn't silence the voice in her head any longer. There was only one, big reason a single man takes a woman to a motel. He hadn't denied it when she asked if he was married. He'd simply paused at the door for three heartbeats before leaving.

The guilt she'd experienced at that moment resurfaced. She hadn't known he was married. But that didn't change the fact that for a single night, she was the other woman.

Her husband Levi ended their two-year marriage for another woman. The woman he had been sleeping with their entire marriage. It hadn't occurred to Alison until that moment, lying in a pile of cheap motel sheets and feigning sleep while she watched Jerimiah dress, that the woman who had been sleeping with her now ex-husband might have had no idea he had been married.

She squeezed her eyes shut as she fought with her traitorous mind not to think about Jerimiah's wife, his family. It wasn't until a month later that she discovered he had left her with more than a lackluster memory. Those two pink lines on the pregnancy test had been a blessing.

She drew in a breath. There was no way Ronan would understand her hesitation at letting another man into her life. No one was sexier than him with those broad shoulders, genuine smile, and pierced nipples. He would bring in a lot of money for the Children's Hospital.

She couldn't fault him for auctioning off his New Year's Eve kiss to another woman. The man had tried to kiss her all night.

CHAPTER THIRTEEN

Ronan leaned against the bar. "Hey, Joey."

Joey flipped a bottle of whiskey around in his hand. "Need another drink?"

Ronan shook his head. "Nah, I hit my limit a couple beers ago. Thanks, though. Have you seen Alison? We're closing in on midnight and she promised me a kiss."

Joey hesitated and alarm shot through Ronan. "Did she leave? Shoot. I don't have her number. Help me out?"

Joey shook his head. "I don't think she would be okay with that, man."

Ronan nodded. "Yeah, you're right."

Ronan turned and scanned the crowded room for Alison. Something was wrong. Earlier, she had broken off their dance before the song ended, but the way she'd moved on the dancefloor had been pure sex. He'd lost track of her about a half hour ago and hadn't been able to tear himself away from the photo ops and autographs to find her.

"She doesn't really know me," Ronan said over his shoulder. "Wait." He faced Joey. "What did she say?"

Joey raised a brow. "You're taking part in the New Year's Eve Kiss Auction, aren't you?"

Ronan frowned. Then understanding struck. "Fuck."

"Yeah."

Ronan closed his eyes, wishing he hadn't volunteered for the auction. "How mad is she?"

"Not so much mad as disappointed," Joey said. "A lot embarrassed, I would guess."

Guilt stabbed him. "So, she left?"

Joey grabbed a frosted beer glass from the fridge and pulled the Budweiser lever on the tap. "She's here. She's just an expert at avoiding men she doesn't want to be around."

"And that's me, isn't it?"

Joey shrugged. "What can I say?"

Ronan rubbed the back of his neck. "Okay. If that's all that is bothering her, I can fix it. Help me get out of this kiss auction."

Joey set the beer on the empty tray sitting on the counter. "Can't. It's for the kids. Megan would kill me."

"Shit, okay. How much do you think this kiss will go for?"

"A couple hundred, maybe."

Ronan nodded. He didn't really need that second tattoo of black and grey flames on his calf, though he'd been saving for months. "I'll pay for it."

Joey's brows shot up. "For your own kiss?"

"Exactly."

"Hey, Ronan." His sister stepped up beside him and smiled.

He knew that smile. Just what he needed tonight, more trouble.

"Kelly Ann—" he began and dropped onto a barstool.

"Would you say Diego is a nice guy?" she cut in.

"Diego Fuentes?" Ronan frowned. "From my firehouse?"

She nodded. "Yeah. Mr. November."

"No."

She shoved his chest. "Come on."

"He's my age." His voice was embarrassingly high.

"And?"

"And men in their twenties don't spend time at church picnics and knitting circles."

"In case you haven't noticed, Ronan, I don't spend my time at church picnics and knitting circles."

Ronan shook his head. "I work with the guy, Kel."

She rolled her eyes. "Stop being a baby. I'm an adult, and he's really cute."

"He's seven years older than you. That's a lot of life experience he has on you."

"Maybe that's a good thing?"

Ronan didn't want to think about his sister's sex life. Joey's snort of laughter from behind the bar only reinforced his decision. "No. It's not. Aren't there any nice freshmen at college?"

"I'm probably not even his type," she said. "I'm not the typical knockout, you know?"

"Hey, now. Kelly Ann. I didn't say that. You are beautiful. Inside and out."

Her growl could be heard over the music of the juke box and the din of the crowd. His sigh was not much quieter as he watched her march away. Toward the firefighters' table. Toward Diego.

"Hey, Joey," a guy called from the other end of the bar. "A round of tequila shots, over here."

Joey nodded, grabbed a bottle of Jose Cuervo from the shelf behind him, then faced Ronan. "Kids, huh?"

Ronan blew out a breath. "Teenagers. You have kids?"

"Hell no. I can't. Afghanistan." Joey set the tequila on the counter and grabbed four shot glasses from the overhead shelf.

"Oh, Jesus. Sorry, man."

Joey shrugged. "Megan considers all the kids at the Children's Hospital as her own. It's the reason tonight is so important to her."

"Wow. She's a saint."

"She's a lot of things." Joey smiled in the direction of his wife who stood at the cash register. "A saint is definitely one of them."

"Look, I need to fix things with my sister." Ronan stood. "We're still on for the New Year's kiss plan, right?"

Joey nodded. "Yeah. I'll help you out. But if Alison is pissed, you get all the blame."

Ronan reached across the bar to shake Joey's hand. "Deal."

"How much you willing to pay?" Joey asked.

"However much it takes."

Cara's cry yanked Ronan's attention in her direction. "Let go of me, you pervert."

A bulky, middle-aged man gripped Cara's arm near one of the rear booths.

Ronan pushed through the crowd toward the bastard.

"Mr. July? Will you sign my calendar?" a female voice called out as Kelly Ann jumped to her feet beside Cara.

"Five minutes, sweetheart," he said, and continued toward Cara.

"Just dance with me, baby." The man yanked Cara against him.

Diego reached them two seconds before Ronan did. "Hey, bro. Fuck off."

The man sneered. "You think that, just because you're firemen, you're better than the rest of us?"

"It actually does," Kelly Ann said.

Ronan pushed her back behind him and stepped toward the guy.

"Sir." Their lieutenant stepped in front of Ronan. "This young woman clearly isn't interested. Let her go."

"She looks interested to me," he said.

Cara pinched his arm.

The man jerked. "Bitch."

"That's enough." Joey pushed past Ronan. Out from behind the bar, the guy was huge. It was obvious he was former military. "Get out of my bar."

"I'm a paying customer," the man replied, but his eyes remained locked on Ronan.

What the hell?

Ronan had never seen this man in his life. But the man knew him.

The guy shoved Cara toward Diego, then lunged at Ronan, swinging a fist. Ronan dodged the guy's fist and stumbled aside. He bumped into Keith, who knocked Kelly Ann to the floor.

Ronan righted himself and rammed his fist into the guy's jaw. The man drew back his fist, but Joey grabbed the loser by the collar and dragged him toward the door.

"I don't want to see you around here again," Joey shouted as someone opened the door. "Next time, I call the police." Joey shoved the guy outside.

The crowd cheered when the door closed. Joey limped back to the bar, waving off the applause.

Ronan faced his sister and Cara. "Are you two all right?"

Kelly Ann's eyes flashed. "That guy was a jerk."

Ronan's jaw tightened. "This is a perfect example of why you two shouldn't be here."

Kelly Ann rolled her eyes. "Women of all ages meet jerks."

He raised a brow. "Yeah, but older women are better prepared for situations like that."

"It wasn't their fault." Diego wrapped his arm around his sister's shoulder.

Ronan shot him a thin-lipped look. "She isn't your sister, Diego."

Diego lifted his hands, palms up, in a motion of surrender.

Kelly Ann stepped between them and narrowed her eyes on Ronan. "Stop acting like a jerk, Ronan McGuire, or I'll tell Grams."

Ronan blinked. "What?"

"You're not too big for her to take you over her knee."

Diego snorted a laugh. Ronan shot him a warning glance.

Alison appeared at his side.

"How's your hand?" She held a wet towel full of ice as a makeshift ice pack.

Ronan looked at her in confusion.

She smiled gently and lifted the towel and ice. "Your hand?"

He looked down at his hand and flexed his fingers. They would hurt in the morning. "Yeah, all good. Thanks, though." He glanced at the door. Who the hell was that guy?

"Ronan. Let him go," Alison said.

He nodded, his gaze still on the door. "Wait for me." He glanced at her and smiled, then headed for the door. "I'll be right back."

A moment later, he pushed through the door and stepped out into the cold December air. Wind whipped at the sweat-dampened locks on his forehead. A rusted brown station wagon peeled out of the lot before he had a chance to read the plates.

Movement across the lot caught his eye. A broad-shouldered man dressed in black with a hood pulled up over his head stood in the shadow. Something about the guy seemed familiar.

When Ronan started toward him, the man spun and hurried away. Ronan halted and rubbed his right knuckles until the man disappeared into the darkness.

After a final visual sweep of the packed parking lot, Ronan turned and reentered the bar. He found Kelly Ann sitting on

Diego's lap at the firemen's table. She smiled shyly at something he said. Cara laughed with Keith, and, of course, Mike was there.

Ronan let out a deep breath and started toward the table. Intellectually, he knew she wasn't a kid anymore, but damnit, this night had been a real wake up call.

When he reached the table, Kelly Ann jumped up and threw her arms around Ronan's neck. "I forgive you." She kissed his cheek and added, "Thanks for protecting us."

He shook his head. "Oh, you're good."

CHAPTER FOURTEEN

As Alison waited at the bar for her order to be filled, Megan left the cash register and halted beside her. "He's been looking for you."

"Mr. July?" The handsome man who had given her hope for the first time in months.

"Oh, yeah." Megan flashed those all-knowing eyes at her.

Alison shook her head. A girl couldn't keep a secret around here. "I'm bummed, Meg."

"Babe, I know. I get it. It's my fault he's doing the New Year's Eve Kiss Auction. Blame me."

"No. I understand. He was sweet to sign up for the auction. He's going to bring in a bunch of cash for your kiddies."

"But..." Megan urged.

"But I wish it was me kissing him at midnight."

"That so?"

Alison shook her head. "I'm being stupid. I turned him down all night. What did I expect?"

"You just work your cute little bum off while I go do this auction, and maybe you won't notice some rich old granny making out with Mr. July."

Alison ignored the stab of jealousy and smiled. "Is that your way of telling me to get back to work?"

"You know it." Megan winked, then headed to the table of firefighters.

Alison faced the bar. Men only brought trouble. Especially a hot, sexy man with massive biceps and a tight ass. A man who made her feel desirable for the first time in longer than she could remember. Jerimiah had made her feel wanted, but that desire had been tainted by his deceit.

"I'll kiss you at midnight," Joey said, setting five beers and a dirty shot on her tray. "On the cheek. That still counts."

She grimaced. "The only thing worse than no kiss on New Year's Eve is a pity kiss."

"I have to disagree, Miss Walker. My lips saved an entire overseas platoon once."

Alison lifted her brows. "Oh, really?"

"I'll tell you the story sometime. You would be amazed. And you would also think twice about turning down my kisses."

Alison shook her head and caught sight of Ronan across the bar talking to a sexy woman in a tight, leopard print dress. He was so handsome—and the woman was hanging on his every word. Maybe she would be the one to win Ronan's kiss.

RONAN'S eleven calendar brothers continued to dance like the night was young. Ronan sat at the table nearest the stage in hopes that he was invisible to the throngs of increasingly drunk women. Midnight couldn't arrive soon enough. He wanted to kiss Alison, no matter the cost.

"Hey, McGuire."

Ronan glanced up from the drink he didn't order and smiled

at Janis, still stunned at how feminine she looked out of uniform.

She narrowed her eyes. "I don't look that different. You can stop staring."

"I honestly didn't recognize you earlier. You look great, Janis. I didn't realize your hair was so long."

"Don't remind me of that horrible haircut I had in high school." She touched her hair as if to make sure it wasn't that short anymore.

Ronan had always thought her bob was cute, but she'd hated it the minute she got it.

"Anyway, I didn't come over to reminisce," she said. "I had a thought about the recent fires."

He straightened. "Wait. Fires? Plural? Have you found a connection between the fires?"

"Don't gloat, McGuire. We are looking into a possible arson."

"You just made my night, Janis."

"I didn't come over here to stroke your ego." She pulled up a chair and sat down. Janis reached for his beer, then hesitated and redirected her hand to her belly. "Shoot. The baby."

"Let me order you a ginger ale," Ronan offered.

Janis shook her head. "No, thanks, I'm fine. I came to ask some questions."

"Questions?" he snorted. "Unlike you, I've had a lot to drink tonight."

She nodded, but her expression sobered. "This is important. Think about your training and coursework. Any classes you took to meet qualifications."

He leaned back in his chair. "Okay."

"Think about your fellow students, fellow applicants. Maybe anyone who hangs around the station or inserts themselves in the scene of a fire." She brushed her long hair back over her shoulder.

Ronan frowned. "You think the arsonist is a fireman?"

She shrugged. "It's more common than you think. I have a theory the suspect could be someone who didn't make the cut. Jealousy is a powerful motive."

"I've known several guys over the years who didn't make the cut."

Janis gave a slow nod. "This would be someone who was... off somehow, and they're probably someone more recent in time, say, the last year."

Someone who was off...

Ronan closed his eyes and tried to ignore the noise. No easy task, considering all the free beer that coursed through his blood and clouded his head. He filtered through the names: Robertson, Morris, Haywood...Williams. Five—no—four months ago, Ronan had been paired with Williams for training. His booming voice was a disruption to the class. He was a know-it-all with a barrel chest and twenty-inch biceps.

The instructor reviewed the drill: climb the ladder to the third floor, find the victim, load them in the basket using the rocking technique, then lower them safely to the ground on the ladder. It sounded straightforward, but the training involved real smoke and real fire.

Ronan recalled his nerves. Williams, however, stood stock still, eyes locked on the flames. Ronan thought he glimpsed Williams smile behind his breathing apparatus. Before he could be sure, the instructor blew the whistle and Williams shot across the parking lot toward the ladder.

Ronan followed him up the truck ladder and through the snaking hallway to the back rooms of the apartment.

"In here."

Ronan saw the leg of the dummy in a bedroom Williams

walked past. Why hadn't he stopped? Ronan laid the bucket stretcher down and looked up to see Williams standing in the doorway, watching the flames by the window.

"Williams," he called. "Give me a hand."

Williams jumped into action. The rest of the drill went off without a hitch, and Ronan wrote off Williams' behavior as nerves. By the time the next training session rolled around, Williams had quit the program.

Ronan focused his eyes on Janis. "Jason... No, Jenson Williams. He was in a training class about four months ago. He was good, too. Big guy. In shape."

"What makes you think of him?" she asked.

Ronan took a sip of his beer. "At the time, I blew it off as nerves, and I didn't think a thing of it. But—this is gonna sound weird—I could swear he smiled while staring at the flames."

Janis's brows shot up. "He was smiling? And staring at the flames?"

Ronan nodded. "Oh, yeah. He was definitely staring at the flames. I can't be one hundred percent positive he was smiling—he was wearing a mask. That's what I thought I saw, though. The following week, he just wasn't there." Ronan paused. "Now that I think of it, psych exams took place that week."

Janis nodded slowly. "Jenson Williams, you say? I'll call in the name tonight."

"Never take a night off, do you?" Ronan asked.

"Neither do you, McGuire." She stood, and he started when she leaned in and kissed his cheek. "Thank you for your charity work tonight."

He smiled. "All I'm doing is drinking."

"If anything comes of the lead on Williams, I might need you to come down to the station for a statement."

"Sure thing. Let me know one way or the other, will you? O'Malley won't tell me anything."

Janis laughed. "I don't think anyone says no to you, McGuire."

He watched her walk back to the bachelorette party. "You would be surprised."

"Nothing would surprise me with you, Mr. July," said a familiar voice behind him.

Ronan looked over his shoulder and smiled at Alison, who hurried past with a tray of drinks. She stopped at the next table and distributed the cocktails.

When she whirled and neared his table, he said, "That was about work."

"Mm hmm," she intoned as she whisked past.

"Alison," he called, but she was already two tables away.

He sank back into his chair. Damn.

CHAPTER FIFTEEN

"Okay, ladies," Megan's voice boomed over the microphone. "Only fifteen minutes left until we ring in the New Year, and we have three available bachelors who happen to be looking for a kiss."

The crowd roared, and Alison tried to ignore what was happening on stage while she passed out the drinks on her tray.

"Mr. August, Mr. December, and Mr. July."

Alison couldn't help but look. Tanned and young, Ronan looked like all the summertime memories she wanted to make but probably wouldn't. He looked adorably embarrassed. Too damned attractive.

"If you lucky ladies want to share a kiss with one of these handsome men, you must dig deep in your pocketbooks. All the money goes to The Rapid Falls Children's Hospital." Megan faced the men. "We'll start with you, Mr. August."

Wolf whistles and shouts of "He's mine!" and "Take it off, baby!" filled the air.

Mike thrust his thumbs under his turnout suspenders, dragged them down his muscled arms and ran his hands over his bare chest.

"Oh, God," one woman shouted.

Megan laughed. "Mike here is the life of the party, and by the way he flirts, we can all agree he must be a phenomenal kisser."

Louder shouts and hoots rocked the room. Some women jumped to their feet. For an instant, Alison thought they might storm the stage.

"Mike," Megan said. "Tell us about your kissing style."

Alison couldn't help laughing when Diego jumped to his feet and shouted, "Yeah, Mike. Tell us about your kissing style."

"Yeah," the rest of the guys of the fire department shouted.

Mike leaned close to the microphone and said, "I kiss better than you did at CPR training last month."

Uproarious laughter went up.

Mike turned his attention to Megan. "Well," he said, voice far huskier than when he had answered Diego, "I'm an adventurous lover."

"Whoa," Megan said into the mic with a laugh. "We're not going that far. We'll start the bidding for a kiss with this adventurous hunk at one hundred dollars."

"Me." A smiling young blonde at a table near the left wall of the pub waved several bills in the air.

"Two." A middle-aged woman from the bachelorette party table shouted.

Alison laughed. The second bidder was the bride's mother.

"All right," Megan said. "We have two hundred. Anyone want to go for two hundred and fifty?"

"Three," the blonde shouted.

Megan swung her arm in a downward motion. "Going once. Twice." She paused for two heartbeats, then shouted, "Sold for three hundred dollars."

The woman screamed with pleasure.

Alison wound her way through the tables to the bar where

Joey was pouring two glasses of champagne. She set her tray on the counter and blew out a breath. "Can you believe three hundred bucks to kiss a stranger?"

"You would be surprised what people will do for a first kiss, Ali."

She thought of Ronan. Had he really been trying to kiss her in the office? Warmth rippled through her at the memory of his broad, tanned chest inches from her face.

Alison jarred from her thoughts when Joey set the two flutes of champagne on her tray. "Take these to the new love birds, please."

Alison glanced at the bottle. "Oh, Joey. *Bollinger*. Nice."

"You know I'm a good guy." He puckered his lips at her. "I'm here if you need a kiss, too."

Alison gave an exaggerated roll of her eyes, then picked up the tray and headed toward the lucky winner and her prize. The loaded blonde had already wrapped herself around Mr. August. He grinned, clearly thrilled to be hugged by a pair of breasts.

Alison stopped beside them and set the drinks on their table. "Compliments of the house to toast the New Year."

"Thanks, Alison." Mike winked. "Think I'll beat your boy?"

"He's not *my boy*."

He lifted a brow. "Okay."

Alison startled at the stab of sadness to her heart but smiled. "Have a nice kiss, you two."

She continued to deliver drinks as the crowd began to bid on Mr. December. He flexed and posed, causing the women's screams to nearly pierce Alison's eardrums. The bidding reached three hundred and fifty dollars. The winner turned beet red as Mr. December descended the stage.

"Three fifty. Can you believe I beat Mike?" Mr. December asked when Alison arrived at his and the cute brunette's table with their champagne.

Alison smiled at the flushed woman at his side. "Absolutely. I think Mike is all talk."

"All right ladies," Megan said. "Our last set of delicious lips is up for auction."

Alison reached the bar and turned toward the stage where Ronan stood beside Megan. Her breath caught. Had he winked at her?

"Hi. I'm Ronan." He waved and a collective swoon swept the crowd.

"Mr. July," Megan said, a mile-wide smile on her face. "Describe your kissing style."

He laughed and ran his fingers through his hair.

The breath he released into the microphone caressed Alison like velvet. "I like to take my time. Follow your lead."

"You hear that, ladies?" Megan said. "He's a giver."

The crowd whooped their approval.

"Do I hear one hundred, ladies?" Megan asked.

Three hands shot up in the crowd.

"The pretty woman in red was first," Megan said. "How about one fifty?"

Alison's pulse picked up speed as the bidding hit two hundred, then three, then four...

"Last call for four fifty?" Megan's voice was like that of a judge about to deliver the verdict.

Alison glanced from the curvy blonde at table nine, who had bid four hundred, to the stunning redhead in the front row—the one who had been flirting with Ronan during the calendar signing. Would she bid another fifty dollars?

"Five hundred," called a familiar male voice behind Alison.

Alison whipped around. "Joey?"

He shrugged.

"What are you doing?" she demanded.

"I'm bidding."

"Sold for a whopping five hundred dollars to my husband, Joey, who has some explaining to do," Megan called out amidst the laughter of the crowd.

Alison blinked. "Joey?"

Her best friend ignored her and filled a thin flute with the expensive champagne, the other with club soda.

Ruby stepped up beside her, tray tucked under her arm. "I can't wait to hear what this is all about."

Alison stared at Joey, waiting for an answer. Had he lost his mind? She jumped when Ronan stepped up beside her.

"Thanks, man," he said as he picked up the glass of champagne.

Alison snapped her head up to meet his gaze. "I don't get it."

Ronan shrugged. "I wanted control of my own New Year's Eve kiss." He clinked the base of the champagne flute to the glass of club soda, then downed the drink.

Joey frowned. "That's *Bollinger*, not a shot of tequila."

Ronan looked sheepish. "Whoops."

"Five minutes until midnight, ladies and gents." Megan's voice boomed over the microphone. "I want to thank you all for spending the night with us. I'm overwhelmed with the support for the Rapid Falls Children's Hospital. Many thanks to the handsome men of the Rapid Falls Fire Department for giving up their last night of the year and for being such amazing sports here at Andie's. Let's give them a big round of applause."

Applause, whoops, cheers, and whistles reverberated through the bar.

Ronan shifted, and Alison froze when he bent and touched his mouth to her ear. "Listen."

Gooseflesh raced across her arms.

He placed a hand on her hip. Alison turned in his arms and looked up into his eyes. His gaze dropped to her mouth, then snapped back to her eyes.

"I need to kiss you, Alison."

He leaned closer. Heat radiated off his body.

"Twenty," the crowd chimed in. "Nineteen. Eighteen."

Ronan bent and his mouth almost brushed hers.

"It's not midnight," she breathed.

Ronan gave a low laugh. "I paid five hundred dollars for this kiss. It's going to last, gorgeous."

It was her turn to laugh.

"Stop laughing. I want to kiss you."

"Fifteen," the crowd chanted.

She bit her lip. He pressed his lips first to one corner of her mouth, then the other.

"Twelve," the crowd shouted.

She closed her eyes as his warm mouth caressed her cheek for what seemed an eternity.

"Ten," the crowd whooped.

When his lips touched below her ear, a shiver rippled through her.

"Nine."

He kissed her collarbone. She bit her lip.

"Eight."

His mouth slid higher to the racing pulse point on her neck.

"Seven."

When he nipped her earlobe, she tightened her grip on his arm.

"Six."

Her body hummed in response to his touch. He drew back, and she opened her eyes in surprise. He cocked a brow. His expression seemed to say, *If you let me, I'll explore your body inch by inch until I find every spot that makes you shiver.*

"Three," the crowd shouted.

His thumb brushed the line of her jaw.

"Two."

He leaned closer. Her heart pounded.

"One."

"Happy New Year, Alison." His words kissed her lips in the instant before his mouth covered hers.

Alison leaned into him. His arms tightened around her, his chest muscles hard against her breasts. She started when his tongue flicked her lips. Her head spun. She opened and his tongue slid inside. He tasted of champagne. His tongue tangled with hers, and Alison slipped her fingers into the soft hair at the nape of his neck.

Ronan pulled back all too soon. He smiled down at her, then pulled her closer. Everything about him was hard. She didn't know if she was supposed to say something witty or sexy or seductively to make him kiss her again and again and never stop.

Ronan made the decision for her with another kiss.

CHAPTER SIXTEEN

THE HOUR NEARED 2 A.M. THE GUESTS HAD FILTERED OUT of Andie's, leaving the fire department and staff. Ronan much preferred this setting to the crowded bar—though the smaller crowd made it impossible to ignore his baby sister cuddling up to Diego's chest. He would never get used to that.

Alison headed their way from the bar with a tray in hand.

Ronan jumped to his feet. "Come on, let's get this table cleaned." He grabbed several glasses and winked at Alison as he strode past her toward the bar.

She shook her head, but he glimpsed the smile that tugged at her lips. Within minutes, they had their table and three others cleared.

Keith stretched his arms over his head. "Let's clear out, men, so the Andrews can lock up. You may have tomorrow off, but I have a week's worth of paperwork waiting for me on my desk."

The squad filtered out of the bar, but Ronan hung behind and helped Alison and the other waitresses wipe tables.

"Time to get my lady home," Joey said, at last. "Ruby and Roxy, I'll walk you to your cars."

They didn't wait to be told a second time and said their goodbyes.

Joey left with them, and Alison and Megan continued to wash glasses.

When Joey returned, he said, "No more cleaning tonight, Alison. You want to lock up?" He looked at Ronan. "If your friend plans on seeing you to your car, that is."

"That's the plan," Ronan said before Alison could protest.

Alison rolled her eyes in mock reprimand, but her cheeks pinked before she turned to Megan. "Have fun with your soldier, Meg."

"I always do." Megan and Joey waved goodbye and left.

Alison continued to wipe down the counter behind the bar.

"Joey said you didn't have to clean," Ronan said.

She laughed. "He says that because he knows I will."

Ronan sat on a stool at the bar. He didn't want the night to end. He wanted to go home with her and spend more time with her. "Do you need to get back to Emmy?"

"She's at my mom and dad's. I'll pick her up in the morning."

Ronan wanted to offer her a ride home, but he had drunk far too much. He jumped up from the stool. "I'll give you a hand." He hurried behind the bar where dirty glasses still remained in the sink.

"You don't have to do that," she said.

"Sure, I do." He winked, then turned to the sink and rolled up the sleeves of his RFFD sweatshirt. Someone had made off with his t-shirt after Alison tossed it into the crowd.

Alison was quiet while he washed the first glass, then asked, "Why did you become a firefighter?"

He blew out a deep breath and shook his head.

She took the glass from his hand and began drying it. "You don't have to tell me."

He looked into the soapy water inside the sink. "When I was twelve, my parents were killed in a restaurant fire. They had gone out to dinner for their fifteenth wedding anniversary. Dad wanted to wine and dine Mom. He was a romantic.

"There was a grease fire in the kitchen," he went on in a quiet voice. "A crew of firemen were the first on the scene." He cleared his throat before continuing.

"The police told us my parents were dead on arrival, but the fire crew went inside to make sure there were no survivors. I admired them for that."

Alison set the glass down and took his soapy hand in hers. "I am so sorry."

He forced a smile. "I'm sorry. That was a lot to unload on you."

"No. I appreciate you trusting me with that."

His smile came easy this time. "I'm an open book. Ask me something else, Alison."

"Okay. Why me?"

He frowned. "Why did I kiss you? That's an easy one. I like you."

Alison smiled. "Well, I like you too, Mr. July. Did you choose to flirt with me because I looked like an easy target?"

His expression sobered. "At first. I was at the bar to grab a couple beers for the guys, nervous as hell about this event, still stressed from the fire call we had earlier. And then I saw you standing there. Sexy as sin in those heels." He winked. "I thought, wow, this girl is gorgeous. Then I just opened my mouth." He shrugged. "So, yes, I was—am—very attracted to you. I sought you out afterwards to apologize, though. That isn't the kind of guy I am."

"I can tell."

He leaned in and brushed his lips across hers. "What keeps me coming back, Alison Walker, is the real you. Your sarcasm. I adore your love for Emmy, your protective nature, your pride in who you are and what's important to you. Your loyalty to your friends. We're similar in a lot of ways. So"—he pointed his finger between the two of them—"if you're asking if this could have happened with anyone else here tonight, any night, for that matter, I would have to say no."

"I think I like that answer."

Ronan laughed. "It's the truth."

Alison bit her lip, then shook out the towel she'd used to dry the glasses. "It's time to get out of here. I'll get my purse from the office." She looked up and smiled at him with tired eyes.

He would give anything to stop this night from ending. The way she looked at him, with just a hint of desire in her smile, told him she didn't want the night to end, either.

Ronan resisted the urge to take her in his arms and smiled. "Sure."

He watched the sway of her hips as she walked toward the office. Fuck, he had it bad. Ronan leaned forward, forearms on the countertop. Though he was beat, he would stay up all night, even if she just wanted to talk.

His mind snapped to attention. Was that gasoline?

Another whiff of the too-familiar smell. He had to get to Alison.

CHAPTER SEVENTEEN

RONAN STOPPED DEAD AT THE HALLWAY ENTRANCE. His nostrils burned with the reek of gasoline. Fear lanced through him.

"Alison?" Smoke streaming from under a door at the far end.

He drew in a deep breath and headed to the door. He touched a finger to the door and yanked back when the metal burned his skin. He grasped the knob with the end of his shirt and turned. A wave of blistering heat rolled through the opening. Ronan threw up a hand and blinked against the sting of smoke. Through the partially open door, he spotted orange flames engulfing the room. Boxes of napkins and straws burned.

Dread zipped up his spine. This fire was no accident. Was it connected to the other fires now suspected of being arson?

It was if Jenson Williams was involved.

The fire leapt toward the door.

"Fuck." He yanked the door closed.

If the flames breeched the door, the gasoline would set the hallway on fire in seconds. Where was Alison? His gaze caught on the small alcove to the right where the restrooms were located. The ladies room. He lunged and burst inside.

"Alison!" The door crashed against the wall in unison with his shout

"Ronan?" Her voice emanated from the middle stall.

"There's fire in the storeroom. We need to get out of here." He looked around the room for an exit. One window, too high and too small to escape through. "*Now*."

The stall door opened and Alison emerged, tugging down her dress. "What are you talking about?"

He grasped her hand and pulled her to the exit, then stopped short at the sight of smoke seeping under the door. How the hell had smoke gotten into the hallway so quickly?

Alison gasped. "Oh my God. What are we going to do?"

"Get the hell out."

Ronan stripped off his sweatshirt and crossed to the sink.

"How?" Alison hugged herself.

He soaked the sweatshirt under cold water, then twisted off the faucet, thrust the wet shirt in Alison's hand and swung her into his arms. She cried out and threw her arms around his neck.

"Put the shirt over your head," he ordered.

"Ronan—"

"Do it."

She hesitated, then covered her head with the wet shirt and buried her face in his neck. Ronan drew in a deep breath and opened the door. Smoke poured into the restroom. He lunged into the hallway.

His heart jumped into his throat at the loud, haunting moan of destruction emanating from the direction of the storage room. Angry flames licked a destructive path along the ceiling and walls. Toxic, black smoke rolled down the hall toward the exit. His blood ran cold. The only way the fire would have reached the hallway in such a short time would be if someone had still been in the bar and had thrown a match into the gasoline.

Alison clung tighter and he hugged her closer. Heat

scorched his bare neck and back. His eyes were focused on that one spot of white light ahead of him.

The front door.

They burst into the smoke-filled bar. Flames engulfed a small section of the front counter. Ronan's boot caught on the leg of a chair. He stumbled, drew in a harsh breath, and righted himself. Smoke burned his lungs. He coughed but forced his legs to pump faster.

Alison cried out. His eyes burned so badly his vision blurred. They reached the door. He tried to flip the lock but the door was already unlocked. Someone had been inside the bar. Ronan threw the door open and surged out into the empty parking lot.

Cold air washed over him, and he dragged the fresh air into his burning lungs. He ran another twenty feet, then fell to his knees and yanked the shirt from Alison's head. She gulped in air but didn't cough. Thank God. She hadn't inhaled any of the smoke. Her eyes were wide and wild, her cheeks stained with tears.

"You're okay, Alison." His voice scratched from the smoke. "We made it out. That's all that matters."

She buried her face in the crook of his neck. "Are you all right?"

"More than all right now." He pressed his mouth to her forehead. "I'm damned grateful I stayed behind."

She shivered. "Me, too."

Sirens wailed in the distance, maybe a good two or three blocks away. Ronan looked across the street and saw someone standing in the window of the convenience store. He waved his thanks and the woman waved back.

Seconds later, flashing red lights—the good kind of red lights—bounced off the overcast sky.

The cavalry was on the way.

CHAPTER EIGHTEEN

The mint green hospital gown was a far cry from a cocktail dress. Alison's mascara had run and burned her eyes, and she was connected to a machine that monitored her vital signs—despite her insistence that she felt fine. Well, physically, anyway. She drew in a deep breath. The blaze had surrounded them with an intense heat she hadn't imagined possible.

She started when the heart monitor beside her beeped. Despite the unruly patient behind the curtain across the hall and the nurses discussing medication in the hallway, she felt isolated. Alone.

A pink, plush bunny sat in the visitor's chair in the corner of her curtained off area of the emergency room. Ronan must have delivered it when she drifted off. The sight brought tears to her eyes. Her stay in the hospital was only a precaution. Nothing serious, the doctor had said. Yet her hands hadn't stopped shaking since she'd been put into the ambulance.

The realization of what could have happened had hit hard. She had been embarrassed to cry in front of the paramedics but couldn't stop the tears. She had wanted Ronan to climb into the ambulance with her and hold her hand, but he stayed behind to talk to the firefighters who came to extinguish the fire raging through the roof of Andie's.

"Hey, girly." Megan peaked around the curtain before entering the room with Joey close behind. "How are you doing?"

Alison wiped her nose. "How bad is it? Andie's?"

"The back half isn't too hot right now. But we have insurance," Megan said.

Joey sat on the foot of the bed and squeezed her calf through the blanket. He looked exhausted. Megan's eyes were red rimmed, but the two of them smiled their support.

"Don't worry about the bar," Joey said. "It will be fixed. You're what's important. We're so damn glad you made it out all right."

"I'm fine. I don't even need to be here." Alison sniffled. "I'm so sorry. You left me in charge of Andie's and look at what happened."

"Don't." Joey shook his head. "Don't do that. No blame. It was arson. We were talking to the fire investigator. She said gasoline was used as an accelerant. There was nothing you could have done."

"Still—"

"We're going to rebuild. It will be okay. We're going to be okay. We have money saved and loads of insurance." Megan pulled Alison into her arms.

Alison pushed her hair behind her ear. "Have you seen Ronan?"

"Yes. At the nurse's station." Joey shook his head. "He inhaled some smoke, but he's okay."

"He cares about you," Megan said.

"He would have risked his life for anyone in the fire," Alison said.

Joey shrugged. "So?" He looked at his wife. "As a man who

fell in love at first sight, I can attest to it being a real phenomenon."

Megan rolled her eyes, but Alison could see she was pleased.

Megan patted her hand. "He literally walked through fire to save you. Do you like him—even a little?"

"God, it would be impossible not to like him, but...the fire. The heat. I've never been so scared. He does it everyday. One day, he might not..." She couldn't finish the sentence.

Joey stood and took two steps to the head of the bed, then bent and kissed her forehead. "I was blown up, Alison. I could have been killed on a daily basis when I was overseas. But Megan stayed with me. She's far braver than I could ever be."

Megan rubbed her husband's back. There was no doubt the two of them had been through hell. And it had only made them stronger.

Megan returned her attention to Alison. "You can't control love, babe. If you care for him, you'll care for him for who he is."

Alison closed her eyes for a heartbeat, then opened them and asked, "Did you lose tonight's earnings?"

"Fireproof safe." Joey smoothed her hair back from her face and kissed her forehead once more then stepped back. "Get some rest, Ali."

Megan squeezed her in a tight hug. "We love you. Feel better."

"Again, sorry about the bar."

"Don't be. No one was hurt and, in the end, that's what's important," Joey said.

Alison watched her best friends leave, hand in hand, more in love today than ever. They would be all right.

Her mom burst into the cubicle like a ball of uncontrolled energy, followed by Alison's calm, rational father with a brave face in place. "Sweetie. Are you okay?"

Alison smiled up at her mom. No matter how old a girl was, she would always need her mom. "I'm fine, Mom."

God, she was lucky to have such incredible parents. It didn't matter to her dad she wasn't his biological daughter. He loved her like she was his own.

"I'm sorry Megan called and woke you. I'm okay. I promise. Where's Emmy?"

"Mrs. Wilson from next door agreed to watch her for an hour. You know how she loves babies. Has fourteen grandchildren of her own now." Her mom folded and unfolded the top of the bedsheet. Alison nodded in relief. "That's fine. I like Mrs. Wilson."

"What happened, muffin?" Her dad sat down in the empty chair beside the bunny.

Alison shook her head. "I don't know. I was in the bathroom when one of the firefighters came to get me. The flames"—she swallowed—"moved so fast. He carried me out. I don't think I've stopped shaking."

"Ronan?" Her dad read the tag that hung from the bow around the pink bunny's neck.

Alison's cheeks warmed. "Yes."

"Is he the handsome young man pacing the hallway?" Her mom grinned.

Alison wondered, now that she was a mother herself, if she would perfect that knowing look her mom always wore when she thought she had everything figured out.

"Meg said he was here." Alison smoothed back her hair. "I haven't seen him since they loaded me into the ambulance."

"Following a patient to the hospital? Buying gifts?" He tugged the bunny's ear. "This goes above and beyond the call of duty, doesn't it?" Her dad wore an easy smile. "Is there something we should know?"

Alison ignored the tremor that rippled through her stomach.

"I like him." She didn't want to say too much. It was too soon to say what would happen between them. "Maybe it's too soon to date, though."

Her mom pressed a kiss to Alison's forehead. "I'm sorry, Alison, if I've made life harder for you."

Alison frowned. "What are you talking about? You watch Emmy for me while I'm at work. I couldn't ask for more."

"That's not what I mean." Her mom met her gaze. "I've been judgemental. I wasn't happy when you gave up college to marry Levi. I was upset when you had Emmy on your own. I was proud of you, of course, but more than anything, I was scared. Children are demanding. But you've proven how dedicated you are. Oh, Ali, you have made us so proud."

A new wave of tears slid down Alison's cheeks.

"We don't say it enough, but we love you, kid." Her dad patted her leg. "And it seems someone else is pretty enamoured with you too. Should I get him?"

At Alison's hesitation, her mom smiled. "We'll give you your privacy."

"We will?" her dad asked.

"Daddy," Alison said.

He kissed her forehead. "Call if he's not a gentleman."

"I love you both," Alison said as they left.

She smoothed her unflattering hospital gown. Her hands still shook. Knowing she was about to see Ronan didn't help matters.

CHAPTER NINETEEN

The woman of Ronan's dreams, the woman he was falling for, was asleep in an emergency room.

The hospital was far from his favorite place. Gran had taken him with her to this same hospital after his parents' death. He didn't see their bodies, but he remembered the feeling of dread. The feeling of loss and pure, gut-wrenching sorrow.

There was a reason he chose a career that ended at the ambulance doors.

Tonight, though, he hadn't been able to leave. Not without seeing firsthand that Alison was all right.

He stepped closer to the bed and closed the curtain behind him. "Alison?"

Her eyes fluttered open. Her face was flushed, her hair tangled, and her makeup was smudged around her eyes. Still beautiful.

"Hi," she said. "Thank you for the bunny. It's cute."

"I would have bought you flowers, but the selection at the twenty-four-hour convenience store this time in the morning is lacking."

Her smile came easily. "It's perfect. Would you like to sit down?"

Ronan blew out a deep breath. "I would love to."

Alison laughed. "You need to come closer, then."

"Right." He stepped over to the bed, wiped his palms on the back of his jeans, then sat on the foot of the bed.

"Where did you get the t-shirt?" she asked. Her eyes moved over his chest before meeting his gaze.

"Stan from third watch lent me his." Ronan winked at her. "I think I was showing him up at the scene with my physique."

Alison tugged her hospital gown up in an effort to hide the fact she wasn't wearing a bra.

"Am I making you uncomfortable?"

"No." She shook her head. "I'm just..."

He set his hand on her ankle and squeezed. "What is it?"

"I'm just a bit off my game right now."

"You went through a lot tonight. How do you feel?" he asked.

"The doctor said I'm in shock." She frowned. "God, how are you?"

"Minor smoke inhalation. I'm fine," Ronan said.

"Why aren't you in a bed with an oxygen mask?" she asked.

He laughed. "I know the doctor. I might have bribed my way out."

"Well, now I feel ridiculous," she said. "You had it worse than me, and here I am, still in bed."

"It's important they give you the all clear before you go home," he said.

She seemed more relaxed now, and her calm did wonders for his nerves.

Ronan grasped Alison's hand and gently squeezed. "I'm glad you're okay."

"Thank you." She laughed. "I feel like I owe you a car or something. You saved my life."

"We can't take gifts, Alison."

"What if we don't tell your boss?" she asked, a smile playing on her lips.

"Keith?" He shook his head. "Yeah, he'd notice a new car in the parking lot."

"Well, maybe we can figure something else out." She waggled her eyebrows.

Ronan laughed with her. "Oh, yeah? Like what?"

"Will you kiss me again?" she asked, her voice soft.

"I would love nothing more." He indicated the pale green curtain that surrounded them. "But your parents are right behind this curtain."

"Playing hard to get doesn't suit you, Mr. July," Alison teased.

Ronan looked back at Alison. She wasn't laughing. She appeared on the verge of tears. "What's wrong?" he asked.

"I'm afraid."

He nodded. "Fire takes a bit of getting used to, that's for sure. But I will say, I've never been that scared in my life."

"Really?" Her eyes became wide pools again.

"I had a lot to lose."

She looked down, shyly, and then quickly yanked the hospital blanket up to her neck. "I'm scared of how I feel about you."

Ronan frowned. "What? Why? I would never hurt you."

"What if a fire hurt you?" She paled.

"I'm good at my job, Alison."

She shook her head. "I know. Never mind. I shouldn't have said anything."

Ronan stood and cupped Alison's cheek, looked into her eyes, then leaned in to kiss her.

"Sir, I'd like to give our patient a quick exam before we release her," a male doctor said behind him.

Ronan halted, his mouth a hair's breadth from hers. Alison stared at him, eyes still wide. He winked and caught a hint of the blush that pinked her cheeks in the instant before he straightened and faced the doctor.

"Yes. Of course." He turned toward Alison. "Will you come to dinner tomorrow? Four o'clock at my Grandmother's house. She does a family supper every year on New Year's Day. Tradition. Bring Emmy?"

Uncertainty flickered in her eyes. "Are you sure? Isn't that for family?"

"I have this horrible suspicion Kelly Ann is going to invite my buddy Diego."

She smiled wide. "And you need someone to reign you in?"

"Actually, that's a very good idea." He laughed. "But, really, I want you to be there." He leaned close and whispered, "You're important to me."

"Already?"

"Yes." He kissed her cheek. "I'm glad you're safe." He shot Alison another wink and left.

He reached the waiting room and was surprised when Alison's mom wrapped her arms around him.

"Thank you," she said.

Ronan patted her back and nodded at Alison's father, an older man with salt and pepper hair and an easy smile. "It's my job."

Alison's mother looked up at Ronan as if he was a celebrity. "We're so grateful. Alison is our world."

"I can see why. She's a great girl." He smiled down at her. "Ronan McGuire. I apologize for not introducing myself sooner. It's been a long damn night."

"I'm Trudy. This is my husband, Robert."

Ronan nodded. "Pleasure's mine."

"I'm going to go check on our girl," Trudy said to her husband. She patted Ronan's arm. "Thank you again."

"Sir," Ronan held out his hand to Robert.

"Be patient with her. She's been closed off for so long," Robert said.

Ronan nodded, took that as a father's blessing, and answered truthfully, "I intend to."

CHAPTER TWENTY

Ronan arrived home at four in the morning. He hoped to get in three, maybe four hours of sleep before he headed over to his Grandma's house to help with New Year's Day dinner.

Thank God, he managed to get away with a quick once over from the paramedics at the scene of the fire or he would still be hung up at the hospital with paperwork and a pointless exam.

The lock clicked over on his front door as he turned the key. It had been the best and worst New Year's Eve of his life.

The fire at the bar looked a hell of a lot like the garage fire they had put out earlier that day. Gasoline. He would have to phone Keith and tell him about Janis's theory, about a fireman starting the fire. Or one who didn't make the cut.

"Hi."

Ronan whirled to face his sister. "Jesus, Kelly Ann."

"Sorry. Didn't mean to scare you." His sister lay curled up on his couch, bundled in the blanket he kept there for nights he was too damn tired to make it to bed. Two empty beer bottles sat on the coffee table. *Diego.*

He hung his jacket up on the back of the door and crossed to the couch to sit beside her. She snuggled up against his side, and he didn't hesitate to wrap her in his arms.

"What's going on? Are you all right?" he asked.

"I'm fine." She looked up at him with those big, innocent eyes.

"Kel. Talk to me."

"I wanted to make sure you were okay. We dropped Cara off, then Diego heard about the fire from one of his friends at the station. We drove back and saw the guys from the other crew spraying water on Andie's. I called you, but your phone wasn't on. The ambulances were gone, and I drove to the hospital, but they said you hadn't checked in. So I came here and waited."

"Where's Diego?" Ronan asked.

"He stayed with me for an hour or so, then took a cab home." She smiled. "He says he owes you a few beers."

Ronan raised an eyebrow.

Kelly Ann smacked his leg. "He was a gentleman."

"Mm hmm." He squeezed her hand. "I'm sorry I worried you. I'm okay. Promise."

"Don't lie, Ronan."

He released a breath. "Well, my back is sore, but it's nothing I can't handle."

"Did they give you something for the pain at the hospital?" she asked.

"Don't worry about me," he said. "You girls have a good night? Besides the obvious ending."

"We did. Oh, and I think Cara likes Mike."

Ronan snorted. "All the girls like Mike."

She bit her lip. "I don't."

Ronan lifted a brow. "Want to tell me about that?"

A five-alarm blush appeared on her cheeks and she dropped her face to his shoulder. "Diego kissed me at midnight."

"I figured." But he didn't love the idea.

"You probably didn't notice. You were tonsils deep with Alison."

Ronan took a moment to savor the memory. "Don't change the subject."

"I like him, Ronan."

He nodded. "I know you do."

She met his gaze. "Why don't you want me to date him then?"

"Because you're my baby sister and I don't want you to have sex. Ever."

She slapped his chest. "Ronan. Gross."

"What?" he said in the most innocent tone he could muster.

"We only kissed."

"Keep it that way, huh?" He kissed the top of her head. "I have your back, Kelly Ann. Always. If you ever need me to beat him up, I will."

She twirled her ponytail around her fingers. "I hope I won't have to ask you to do that."

"Diego had better hope I don't." He held her close, as if he could will her to be eight years old again.

"Um,,," She hesitated.

"We don't need to go over the birds and bees talk, again, do we?" he asked in mock seriousness.

She groaned. "Never again. Once was too much."

He laughed. She was right. They had both been so embarrassed, neither of them had spoken of it since. "What's on your mind?"

"I invited Diego to New Year's Day dinner. Grandma said it was okay." She traced the fire department logo on his chest with her fingertip, something she hadn't done since she was thirteen and he had landed the job with the department. "But I can tell him no if you don't want him there. I know New Year's dinner is important to you."

"It's important to me because it was important to Mom and Dad. I want you to have traditions. I want you to have family. Always. But you're eighteen, a freshman in college. I think it's time I allow you to make your own decisions, huh?"

She dropped her head on his shoulder. "I like knowing you're here to look out for me."

"Good, because that's never going to change."

Her expression turned serious and he suddenly realized she really wasn't a little girl anymore. "I worry about you, too."

"Aw, Kel. Never worry about me. I'm too stubborn to get hurt, right?"

She smiled at the line he had been telling her since he started work at the fire department, but he saw the young woman who saw through the lie.

"Did you see Alison at the hospital?" she asked. "How is she doing? I like her."

"I did. She's fine. I like her, too. A lot, actually."

"You should invite her to dinner."

Ronan lifted a brow, glad he was on the same page as his sister.

Kelly Ann nudged him with her leg to make him stand. She rose and tugged the hem of her dress down. "I should go home."

"It's late. Stay here."

She laughed. "Okay. I'll call Grandma. Can I get your bed? It's better than the single in the spare room."

"Sure." He toed off his shoes, pulled his cell phone from his pocket, and set it on the coffee table as he dropped onto the couch. "Just shut off the light, huh?" He stretched out on the couch, sleep already overtaking him.

She leaned over the back of the couch and kissed his forehead. "I love you."

"Love you, too." Ronan smiled when she covered him with the blanket.

"Oh, Mike called," Kelly Ann said.

Ronan sat up. "What? When?"

"About a half hour ago. He said your phone was off, so he called me. Wants you to phone him ASAP. His words."

"Okay. Thanks, Kel."

"Night."

He waited for her to close his bedroom door, then grabbed his phone from the table and thumbed in the code. True to her word, Kelly Ann had called ten times. Diego, twice. Three missed calls from Mike. He'd turned his phone off while at the hospital. Ronan dialed Mike's number.

Mike answered on the first ring. "McGuire, man. You're not going to believe this."

Ronan leaned back on the couch. "You hooked up with someone tonight?"

Mike laughed. "Not the point. I came home to my complex and the garbage cans were scorched."

Ronan straightened. "No damn way."

"Yeah. Old man Harrison from across the alley put the flames out with an expired fire extinguisher." Mike laughed. "You realize he'll never let me live this down, right?"

"He's ninety-two, isn't he?" Ronan asked.

"Ninety-three," Mike said. "He could probably pass the entrance exam."

"And beat your course record, too." Ronan's heart began to pump faster. "We're being targeted, Mike."

"You and me?"

"No. The whole department." Anger swept through Ronan. "That garage fire we put out yesterday, that was around the corner from Peters' house."

"Shit, really?" Mike asked.

"Last month, the fire at the park was right across the street from Trever's place. I'm telling you, this is personal. There was a guy outside the bar tonight watching. I saw him after we threw that dirtbag out."

"Well, be careful, man," Mike said.

"Yeah. You, too."

"Well, at least I have Mr. Harrison watching my back," Mike said.

"Too true. Night, bro."

Ronan set his phone on the coffee table and shut his eyes. His mind churned in overdrive. There was no hope for sleep tonight.

CHAPTER TWENTY-ONE

"How do I look, Emmy?" Alison spun in front of the bedroom mirror and smoothed nonexistent wrinkles from her dress.

Emmy smiled and waved her fists in the air.

"I'll take that as a 'You look great, Mom.'" Alison sat on her bed and slipped on a cute pair of black heels. Meeting Ronan's family seemed like the perfect, important occasion to wear her new shoes.

Minutes later, Alison buckled Emmy into her car seat and gave her a rattle, then slid into the driver's seat. Butterflies skittered across the insides of her stomach. She pulled her phone from her purse and reread the text message Ronan sent that morning.

Happy New Year, Alison. Hope you slept well and you're feeling better. Dinner is at 4 at 35 Fairmont Street.

He was too damn sweet. The butterflies settled down. Alison input Ronan's address into the GPS and turned on the car.

Emmy giggled and played with her rattle as Alison drove across town. "Ma-ma-ma-ma."

Alison glanced at her daughter in the rear-view mirror. Gratitude welled up for her happy, healthy baby.

She turned down Maple Street and slowed when the GPS told her she was approaching the house. Alison caught sight of a large, white house, and her pulse jumped when Ronan stood from the porch swing and started down the half dozen steps to the walkway.

She slowed in front of the curb. "You ready for this, Emmy? I don't know why Mommy is so nervous."

Ronan waved.

Alison put the car into park. "Okay, Emmy. This is it."

Alison turned off the ignition and got out of the car.

"Happy New Year." Ronan met her at the rear passenger door and pressed a kiss to her cheek, a little closer to her lips than was polite. Perfect. She caught a hint of appealing cologne.

"You look beautiful," he said.

She pulled Emmy from the car and ran her hand over Emmy's cheek. "Me or Emmy?"

He was devastatingly handsome in a dress shirt, tie, and dark denim. "Both of you."

"Thank you. You look great." She smiled. "I almost didn't recognize you with a shirt on."

"We can change that." He reached up to loosen his tie. "As your host, I'm here to make you comfortable."

Alison covered his hand with hers. "Don't. I'm teasing. Plus, someone is watching us from the front window."

Ronan laughed. "That would be my sister."

"Oh. Did her beau show up?" Alison asked.

"Diego? Yeah. He's been here for an hour."

"Oh no. Am I late?"

Ronan squeezed her hand. "No, he was just way too damn early. A little overeager, if you ask me."

Alison raised a brow. "So, you sat outside to avoid him?"

Ronan laughed. "I'm struggling with him being here. But I'll be okay. I'm just glad you two beauties made it."

"You're going to make us blush," Alison said.

"You're already blushing. And it looks incredible on you." Ronan leaned in to kiss her cheek once more, then took Emmy's car seat from her. "Come on. Let's get inside. It's cold out."

Alison let out a deep breath and followed him up to the walkway. Twists of multicolored Christmas lights wrapped the banister leading up to the porch, and a large holly berry wreath hung on the solid oak front door.

"You made it." Kelly Ann hugged Alison as she entered the foyer of the overly warm house. Aromas of delicious roast turkey and something sweet like cinnamon filled the house. "You look gorgeous," Kelly Ann said. "I love this dress. Oh my God. Your shoes. Are those..."

"Jimmy Choos?" Alison said. "Yes. My Christmas gift to myself."

"Wow."

"It's a borderline obsession," Alison admitted with a nervous laugh. "Well, maybe not borderline."

"They're amazing," Kelly Ann agreed. "May I hold Emmy?"

"Sure."

Ronan held the car seat steady as Alison lifted her daughter, then laid her in Kelly Ann's arms. "They say, at this age, babies are usually shy around new people, but Emmy loves everyone."

"Ronan," a woman called from the kitchen, "bring Alison over. I want to meet her."

Alison looked at Ronan.

"My Grandma." He set the car seat down on a wooden bench by the door and took her shaky hand. "Relax. We're very down to earth around here."

"Everyone seems great," she agreed.

Ronan stopped in the arched doorway opening into the living room. "Am I making you nervous?"

"A little bit," she admitted.

"It *is* the tie, isn't it?"

She laughed, comforted by his smile and the dizzying scent of his cologne. "Stop threatening to get naked in your grandmother's house."

He laughed. "Crazier things have happened here."

"I'm going to have to hear these stories one day."

"Ronan Patrick McGuire," his grandmother called again.

Alison froze. "Oh, God. I should have brought something. Dessert. I make great cookies."

"No. You shouldn't have," he said. "You were in the hospital until when?"

"Until five this morning," she said.

"There you go. No time for cookies. I'm sure you went home and slept."

She nodded. "True."

"I'm grateful you were feeling well enough to make it today." Ronan led her into the cozy, furniture-filled living room.

A blue-haired woman in a pink, floor-length dress, cinched at the waist, peeked out of the kitchen. Maybe blue wasn't the right word. The seventy-something-year-old woman had the brightest robin's egg colored tresses Alison had ever seen. The only robin's egg colored tresses she had ever seen.

Her smile eclipsed her hair in brightness. "Alison. Sweetheart. You are as stunning as Ronan said." She hurried to greet Alison and enveloped her in a hug.

When the older woman pulled back, Alison said, "Thank you so much for having us, Mrs. McGuire."

"Call me Annie. And is this your sweet baby girl?" She took three steps to the couch where Kelly Ann holding Emmy now sat beside Diego.

"Granny. Look at her." Kelly Ann couldn't seem to stop cuddling the baby.

Emmy giggled and flailed her arms.

Diego smiled at Emmy over Kelly's shoulder, and Ronan's expression turned sober.

"She's sweet as pie." Annie squeezed Emmy's toes. "Alison, will you stir the gravy? I don't want it to burn."

"Of course." Alison turned to Ronan. "Want to keep me company?"

"Most definitely. I'll give you the grand tour." Ronan grasped her hand and led her through the living room to a yellow kitchen, complete with a large round table and pretty, white curtains printed with Holstein cows.

"Quite the tour, Mr. McGuire. Just the two rooms?"

He chuckled. "Growing up here as a teenager, the kitchen was the center of my universe."

"Food on the brain?" Alison teased.

"Among other things, but yes. My grandma is a great cook."

Alison took two steps to the stove, picked up the wooden spoon off the trivet, and stirred the dark gravy. She breathed deep. "This smells incredible. In fact, I can't believe she's letting me interfere with her meal. My mom would never let me cook."

Alison froze when Ronan slid his arms around her waist and pressed his chest against her back. "Grams expects everyone to help out."

"This feels very normal." Her heart pounded.

Ronan nipped at her neck in a way that made her shiver and flush all at once. "Is that bad?" he asked.

"No," Alison answered honestly.

"Too soon?" he asked.

"Maybe. It feels right, but—"

"You don't trust me?"

Alison set the spoon down and turned in his arms. He stared down at her, eyes bright.

"You saved my life," she said. "Of course, I trust you, but I have Emmy to consider."

Ronan traced a finger along her cheek. "I want to be a part of your life—both your lives."

Alison shook her head. "I thought today was hanging out."

He gave her a lopsided smile. "

"There are so many reasons you could change your mind. A whim. Something I say. I'm twenty-three and I still don't know how men think." She shrugged. "Plus, you have a very demanding job. Dangerous, too."

"Men aren't that complicated. We say what we're thinking." Ronan's arms tightened around her. "As for my job, Rapid Falls is a safe town. Last night was an exception." A wicked grin curved his full mouth. "But say the word, and I'll quit and become an accountant."

Alison half grimaced, half laughed. "Fireman to accountant? You would hate sitting at a desk with a calculator."

"I would have to wear a tie every day," he said in mock seriousness. Amusement sparked in his eyes. "We know that ties make you nervous. But yes. For you, I would."

CHAPTER TWENTY-TWO

An hour later, when the meal had finished cooking and everyone had helped Annie carry carved turkey and all the trimmings to the dining room, Alison settled between Ronan and Emmy at the large dinner table. Kelly Ann and Diego sat across from them, and Annie sat at the head of the table to Ronan's left. During the meal, their laughter, clanging of glassware, and the taste and aroma of the many dishes warmed her heart.

"Do you want more turkey, Alison?" Annie asked. "Stuffing? Mashed potatoes? Sweet corn?" Ronan's grandmother laughed. "Don't be shy, sweetheart. We're eaters around here."

"It's true." Ronan loaded his plate with scoop after scoop of cornbread stuffing. "Plus, the food is too good not to eat."

"I'll try the sweet potato pie," Alison said.

"So, it's time for embarrassing stories, right?" Diego asked after swallowing a mouthful of turkey.

"About you?" Ronan asked. "Sure. I'll start. We were at a call last year, and Diego had to sweep the second floor of a residence adjacent to a fire to check for anyone still in the house. We were told there were no pets."

Diego laughed and shook his head. "This is a stupid story."

"Oh," Kelly Ann intoned. "I want to hear it."

"Anyway," Ronan continued, "I'm in the attic, venting the roof where the fire had begun to spread, and I hear this high-pitched scream." He laughed.

"A scared child?" Annie asked, eyes wide. "A trapped woman?"

Ronan nodded. "That's what I thought. So, I race down the ladder, nearly tripping over my damn boots, to help this poor woman in distress. But I find the room empty except for Diego."

"It was you?" Alison turned her head toward Diego.

Diego's face reddened. "I saw a rat."

Ronan winked at Alison, making her shiver in the over-heated house. "It was a mouse. The tiniest mouse I'd ever seen."

"It wasn't that small," Diego said.

"What happened to the little guy?" Kelly Ann asked, fingers gripping Diego's massive forearm. "Did you save him?"

"They had the fire out in ten minutes, and it didn't reach the bedroom. The only damage was to the roof. I'm certain the little varmint is still happily living in the walls of that place," Diego said with a sweet smile.

"Well, that's appetizing." Annie shook her head.

"It's hilarious, Grandma," Ronan said.

"Oh, if you want hilarious," Diego said. "I have a good one about Ronan."

Ronan ran his hand through his long hair and shook his head. "Make sure it's PG."

"Are there stories that aren't PG, Ronan McGuire?" Annie asked. "Because you're not too big to spank, young man."

Alison laughed. Ronan's sweet little grandmother was a tiny thing. Ronan had to be twice her size and the image of her keeping him in line was too cute to imagine.

Ronan leaned in close, brushed her ear with his lips. "Neither are you, Miss Walker."

"Anyway," Diego said with enough glee that Alison figured he intended to exact revenge on Ronan. "We get this call of a trapped man."

"Not this story again." Ronan sighed and took Alison's left hand under the table. He rubbed his thumb over her knuckles. "He tells everyone."

"I haven't heard it," Alison said, melting back into her seat

Ronan looked at her and grinned. Though he'd protested, it was obvious he was enjoying himself.

"So, we get to the apartment, bang on the door, and call out, 'Rapid Falls Fire Department.'" Diego shrugged. "No answer."

"Were you at the wrong place?" Kelly Ann asked, eyes wide and locked on her handsome date.

Alison glanced at Ronan. By the scowl on his face, he had obviously noticed how his sister had her breast pressed against Diego's arm.

She squeezed his fingers. He squeezed back but kept his gaze on his sister.

"Oh, we were at the right place." Diego started laughing so hard he couldn't speak. "The guy just couldn't get to the door."

Alison smiled at Ronan's grandmother. Annie's hand was pressed to her heart and her cheeks were rosy.

"We could hear him yelling," Ronan said, continuing the story where Diego had left off. "So I kicked in the door, thinking he was really hurt."

"What did you see?" Annie asked.

"Far more than we wanted to," Diego said through his laughter.

"We found the guy handcuffed to his bedframe. Legs and arms spread wide open."

Alison choked on a sip of water.

"You okay?" Ronan rubbing his large hand over her back.

She dabbed her lips with the corner of her napkin. "Good. Good. Keep talking."

"Please say he was dressed," Kelly Ann said, cheeks flushed.

"Buck ass naked," Diego said, still laughing. "Looked like he was having a good time too—until his date left."

"That's cruel," Alison said.

"Wait," Annie said. "How did he call the fire department if his hands were cuffed to the bed?"

"Good thinking, Grandma." Ronan pointed at her with his fork. "He didn't call."

"Who did?" Kelly Ann asked.

"We think his lover took pity on him," Diego said. "From a burner phone. Dispatch couldn't trace the call."

"But it was a good damn thing she did," Ronan added. "The guy would have starved to death. He had no friends or family in the area."

"What did you do?" Alison asked.

"Covered his junk with a sheet," Diego said with a snort. "Not that the image isn't burned into my mind."

"I cut the cuffs. It was an easy enough call." Ronan shrugged. "He was treated for minor dehydration and anxiety."

"They didn't catch the woman who did it?" Annie asked.

"No. She robbed him, too," Ronan said. "She cleaned out his wallet and took his watch and a few valuables."

"It was a good lesson." Diego glanced at Kelly Ann. "No cuffs in the sack unless you trust your partner with your life."

Alison looked at Ronan, who stared at Diego.

"Alison," Annie asked. "Do you have any crazy stories about your job?"

"Nothing that can compare to last night," Alison said.

"The room full of firefighters or being carried out of a burning building?" Ronan grinned wide.

"*Half-naked* firefighters," Kelly Ann added.

Alison shook her head. "It was wild. Highs and lows."

"I'm sorry about the bar," Ronan said. "I wish I could have done something to save it."

"No. It's not on you. You are..." Alison smiled. "You were incredible, really. My heart breaks for Megan and Joey, though."

Ronan set his hand on her knee, and Alison looked up when she noticed the laughter had died.

"Oh, God. I'm sorry. This is a happy celebration." Alison shook her head. "Sorry. God. Um. Funny story, funny story. Let me think."

Ronan kissed her cheek. "You don't have to entertain us."

Alison blew out a deep breath. "Wait. I've got it."

Diego nodded. "Lay it on us."

"Okay." Alison glanced from her dozing daughter to Ronan. "I was about two weeks from my due date and still waiting tables. I gained all my weight in my belly but from behind, it was almost impossible to tell I was carrying a baby."

"Nice," Diego said, earning a smack on the shoulder from Kelly Ann.

"Anyway, there was a man at a table in Ruby's section who whistled at me as I walked by." Alison laughed at the memory. "You should have seen his face when I turned around."

"Men aren't into pregnant women?" Diego asked.

"I mean, I had the odd weirdo hit on me, but for the most part, no. Babies aren't a selling point to men on the prowl for a night of fun."

"At the risk of falling into the weirdo category," Ronan said, "I'll bet you looked beautiful."

Annie smiled. "He's a sweet talker, this one."

"He's plain sweet," Alison said.

Ronan smiled and turned in his seat to look at her face. His dark gaze bore into her. She would never be able to hide a thing from this man. Not her fears or her insecurities. A corner of his mouth turned up in a mischievous grin, and Alison realized she'd been staring at his lips.

He winked at her as he rose. "Hold that thought. I'll grab dessert."

FIVE MINUTES LATER, Ronan entered the kitchen and stopped short. Alison's place at the table was empty. He set the pie down near his Grandmother. "Where's Alison?"

"Emmy was hungry. She's in your old bedroom," his grandmother replied.

Ronan nodded. He didn't know the protocol. Should he check on Alison or give her privacy? He had never dated a mom before. Hell. He would check on her.

Ronan left Kelly Ann teasing Diego about wanting two pieces of pie and, a moment later, stopped in front the open door of his childhood bedroom. He grinned at the sight of Alison leaning against the headboard of his bed with Emmy tucked into the curve of her arm and hidden under a pink blanket. Only Emmy's tiny feet stuck out from under the blanket.

Call him a teenager, but seeing a hot girl stretched out on his bed still turned him on. Nevertheless, Alison wasn't a teen girl looking to hook up with the high school bad boy. She was special. She was important. She was breastfeeding her baby girl.

Alison looked. "I didn't mean to interrupt dinner. I usually only breastfeed her in the mornings, but she was fussy. I thought this might do the trick."

Ronan took three steps to the bed and sat beside Alison. He leaned against the headboard, and her bare arm brushed his.

"Don't apologize," he said. "I told you to make yourself at home."

"She's almost finished, and then she'll be ready for a nap."

"Take your time," he replied.

"Ouch." Alison pulled Emmy from her breast and peeked beneath the blanket. "She's teething—which is why I should wean her off breastmilk altogether."

"Yeah? Do babies eat food this soon?"

Alison readjusted the blanket. "Oh yeah. I don't have to breastfeed anymore. It wouldn't be that hard. I make only a little bit of milk, anyway." She sighed. "My mom has been bugging me to wean her. Really makes me mad."

Ronan frowned. "Why?"

"I hate to give up the connection with Emmy, but Mom has always been fairly domineering and puts very high expectations on me." Alison shrugged. "She wants everything done perfectly."

"You're incredible. High expectations are nothing for you."

She laughed. "I'll keep that in mind. I don't totally blame her." Alison leaned her head back against the headboard and closed her eyes. "I don't regret having Emmy, but a one-night stand... Well, let's just say that wasn't my finest hour."

"We've all done it, Alison."

"Maybe, but it's not like I'm eighteen anymore. I should've used better judgement."

"Don't beat yourself up," he said. "And don't let your mom beat you up, either. She's probably just worried about you."

Alison closed her eyes again and nodded. "She is. But I don't need Mom to remind me to not have one-night stands."

"That doesn't mean sex is out of the picture permanently, does it? How does sex work, anyway?"

Her head snapped up.

Fuck, he sounded like a damn teenager. "I—"

"Flunked out of sex ed, did you?" Amusement twinkled in her eyes.

Ronan laughed half in relief. "I'm good, thanks. I, uh, well, I meant sex as a new mom."

She blew out a breath. "Your guess is as good as mine."

His gut tightened. "You haven't—"

"Nope."

That admission pleased him a lot more than it should. "I guess we'll have to figure it out." He waggled his brows. "You know, for science."

She flushed.

Fuck. "I didn't mean tonight."

"Whew." Her lighthearted tone didn't hide her embarrassment.

She reached beneath the blanket and pulled her dress back up over her breast. Ronan tried not to imagine the perfect, erect, rose-colored nipple beneath the blanket—unsuccessfully, of course. His cock began to harden.

Football, he told himself. *Think of football.*

Alison tugged the blanket off Emmy, slung it over one shoulder, then shifted the baby onto her shoulder. She gently rubbed her back.

A strange sense of contentment rippled through him, and he couldn't resist pressing a kiss to her forehead. She looked up at him, uncertainty in her eyes.

His heart picked up speed. No one would hurt her again.

CHAPTER TWENTY-THREE

Ronan's sister filled Alison's mug with more hot cocoa and sat back down at the kitchen table. Emmy was happy as a clam in Annie's arms, and Alison had been trying for the last half hour to ignore the heat radiating from Ronan. He sat too damn close—and she loved it. Alison set down her dessert fork, full after eating a huge slice of pecan pie.

"May I ask you a personal question?" Kelly Ann asked.

Alison wiped her hands and braced for the questions she saw dancing behind Kelly Ann's eyes. "Of course."

"Emmy's dad..." Kelly Ann began.

"Kel," Ronan said, a note of begging desperation in his tone.

Alison placed her hand on Ronan's arm. "Emmy's dad isn't in the picture. In fact, he is so far out of the picture, he's on a different continent."

"Where's he from?" Kelly Ann asked. "Or is it a secret?" Her eyes sparkled as if Emmy's dad was James Bond.

"London, I think," Alison replied "He's married. Megan looked him up online. He has a family. Two kids. A dog." Alison flushed, startled at the honest confession, but she couldn't stop the words. She hadn't had the courage to confess the truth to Ronan earlier when she'd been breastfeeding Emmy.

"He doesn't know Emmy. I used to feel guilty about that," Alison quickly added. "I debated whether or not to contact him. Ultimately, I decided against it. I didn't want to ruin his children's lives. His marriage. I—I didn't know he was married."

No one replied. Oh God, she'd said too much.

Ronan covered her hand with his and gently squeezed. "You have nothing to be ashamed of."

"The man doesn't deserve you," Annie said. "And he most certainly doesn't deserve Emmy. She's far too precious."

Alison hesitated, then said, "I did worry that, if I forced him to be a part of her life, she would grow up around a man who didn't want her in his. That can't be healthy."

"No, it isn't," Ronan's grandmother said.

"Anything else, sis?" Ronan pinned his sister with a hard look.

Her stomach did a somersault when he began tracing circles on the inside of her wrist with his thumb.

"I have a question," Diego said.

Alison tensed. "Sure."

"Can you cook?"

Ronan snorted. "Jesus. This sounds like a perverted job interview."

"I'm a microwave master." Alison winced inwardly, as she thought about the TV dinners and oatmeal she usually cooked. "No, wait. I can cook chili."

Diego laughed. "She's the one, bro."

Ronan pointedly ignored Diego. "Oh, really? Chili, you say?"

Alison smiled with relief at the interest in his voice. "I can teach you how to make it sometime."

"No need. Ronan is the department champ," Diego said.

Alison wanted to laugh. The excitement in Diego's voice gave her the impression that their common love of beans and hamburger was enough to sound the wedding bells.

"He has been working on a secret recipe for the annual state cookoff this summer," Kelly Ann added, a look of pride on her face.

"He's even taking a cooking class at the community college," Annie added with a smile. "He came in second to a veteran from three counties over at last year's chili cookoff."

"Still drives me crazy," Ronan said. "There was too much cumin in Jerry's chili."

Alison laughed. "Well, in that case, I'll bet my chili is horrible compared to yours."

"You know what we should do?" Ronan's eyes sparkled with mischief.

"What?" Alison asked.

"A chili cookoff."

Alison looked over at her daughter perched on Annie's lap, then up at the clock over the sink. "It's nine o'clock at night, Ronan. I need to get Emmy home to bed."

"Friday night? My place?" he said with a wide grin.

Alison grinned back. "You're on."

CHAPTER TWENTY-FOUR

Ronan leaned against the front of his truck parked in the college parking lot. He'd been lucky enough to find a spot right by the door, but with the sheer number of students milling about, he didn't want to miss Alison.

They were meeting on Friday for the chili cookoff in his kitchen, but he hadn't been able to stop thinking of her smile, her green eyes, and—more than anything—those full, luscious lips. Considering he was on leave for a few days and hadn't seen her in two, he had invited her out for coffee. To his relief, she had agreed, and he eagerly awaited their first real date.

He caught sight of her breezing across the common. She wore knee-high boots over tight jeans, a wool coat buttoned to her neck, and a knitted scarf that hid the bottom half of her neck. But she walked with the same energy and confidence that she had at the bar in those sky-high heels.

"Alison." Ronan pushed away from his truck and took a few steps toward her.

She waved, and he smiled as she jogged over to him. She reached him and seemed to hesitate. He grasped her waist and pulled her close. When she wrapped her arms around his neck, he held her tight for a few seconds longer than acceptable.

"It's cold today, huh?" He pressed a soft kiss to her cheek then released her.

"Freezing." She dropped her arms and took a step back, bit her lip as if she were feeling shy. "Thank you for the flowers. They were a nice surprise this morning before class."

"I wanted to let you know I was thinking about you." Ronan opened the passenger side door and grasped her hand as she climbed inside.

"Thanks," she said.

"Of course." He hurried to the driver's side, jumped inside, then cranked the heat up. "Better?"

She nodded. "Much."

"How was class?" he asked.

"It's been a few years since I've been in the classroom, but I guess it's like riding a bike."

"Good." Ronan took her cold hand and rubbed her fingers between his. "What do you feel like doing?"

She gave a small moan that sent a bolt of lust straight to his cock. "That's almost as good as a foot rub," she murmured.

The soft note in her voice made him want to take her in his arms and kiss her until she couldn't think straight. "Maybe one day you'll get to find out how good I am at those, too."

"One day." Alison laughed, her cheeks pink. "I'm starving. Let's eat."

He released her hand and pulled out of the lot. "Do you like Italian?"

"Love it."

He turned left and headed for the south side of the city. "What are you taking this semester?"

"Intro to Business, Intro to Accounting." She laughed. "A lot of intros."

"You have to start somewhere," he said. "Do you like it so far?"

"It's a challenge, but I'm excited. It's a lot different than taking drink orders."

"I bet you have an incredible memory," Ronan added.

"I do."

Ronan laughed. "I'll consider myself warned."

She chatted about Emmy and how Megan and Joey were in the process of finding a contractor to rebuild the bar. Anger swept through Ronan at the memory of Alison in the hospital, how she had been put in danger by the fire, but he forced a neutral expression and asked how the two were doing.

"Pretty good, I guess. Considering."

He nodded and listened as she explained in detail Joey's search for a contractor.

"I don't know this place," Alison said, when he pulled into the parking lot of Mateo's on Third.

He turned off the ignition. "Then you're in for a real treat."

They walked inside, hand in hand, and Ronan watched Alison as she looked around at the small candlelit tables and took in the warm atmosphere.

"Nice place." Alison shrugged out of her jacket and scarf.

"My favorite," Ronan said. "I come here a lot."

"You're too trim to eat that much pasta."

He shot her a wink. "I work out."

Once they were seated at a private table near the back and decided on a thin crust margherita pizza and two root beers, Ronan reached across the table and took her hand once more.

"I've missed you."

She gave him a mock frown. "It's only been three days since dinner at your grandmother's."

He shrugged. "I know."

"You know what, Ronan?"

"What?" he asked.

"I missed you, too."

He held her gaze. "Yeah? Why?"

She leaned back in her seat and crossed her arms over her chest. "I like you—and not just because you're sexy."

"Sexy, huh?"

She rolled her eyes. "You know you're sexy."

He shrugged. "Maybe. But what's important is that you agree."

She blinked, then burst out laughing.

"It's not that funny," he said in mock horror, but he couldn't stop a grin from spreading across his face.

When the waitress brought the pizza, Alison was still laughing, only this time because Ronan had reached beneath the table and tickled her. The waitress set the pizza on the table, and Alison dug in.

Alison glanced up after a few bites. "Sorry. I'm starving. Long day."

"Eat." He took a bite of his pizza. "Now, you were saying something about me being sexy?"

She shook her head and took a long swallow of her root beer. "What do you like, what do you do for fun, and...what makes you mad?"

"What makes me mad?" Ronan knew exactly what made him mad. "Arsonists."

Alison gave a serious nod, and Ronan realized he'd killed the mood.

"What makes you mad?" He took another bite of pizza.

She seemed to consider. "Bad drivers. Oh, and disco music."

Ronan laughed, which was so damn easy to do around Alison. "You haven't seen me dance to *Saturday Night Fever*. I will convert you."

"No." Alison stood and feigned an early exit. "We can't do this."

"I'm teasing. It was a Halloween costume."

"So, costumes are your happy place?" She sat back down and took another bite of pizza.

"That, and cooking, dancing, mini golf." He shrugged. "You know, the usual."

Alison smiled. "Mini golf, huh?"

"Oh, windmills, cheesy black lights, rebound shots." Ronan laughed. "I'm incredibly competitive."

"Cute."

"Wait. I've moved from sexy to cute." Ronan grimaced. "How do we steer this conversation back to sexy?"

Alison smiled at him between bites. "You're a great guy."

"You're a phenomenal woman, Alison."

He noticed her hands tremble as she picked up her napkin. "Nervous?" he asked.

She paused in wiping her mouth and met his gaze. Alison sighed, then set the napkin back on the plate. "That obvious?"

He gave her a gentle smile. "I don't mean to make you nervous. I'm the most laid-back guy in town."

"I don't have a good history with men, Ronan." She shrugged. "I'm a notoriously poor judge of character."

"I'm a great judge of character," he said.

"That's good to know." She picked up another slice.

"All kidding aside, I'm not leaving, and my eyes are only on you."

A blush crept up her cheeks. "Tell me about your past. Your relationships."

He washed down the last bite of his slice, then said, "Well, I dated a lot in high school. I had a girlfriend in college, sweet, but not looking for anything serious. Then, I focused on training and the job."

Her brows rose. "You're telling me you're celibate?"

He laughed. She seemed to always catch him off guard. "I wouldn't say that. But it's been a while. Which means you make me nervous, too."

She cocked her head. "Why?"

He hesitated. "Because you can break my heart, Alison."

"Are you in that deep? Already?" She stared, eyes intent.

"I could be."

She didn't say anything for a long moment. Then she smiled. "Should we get out of here?"

His cock pulsed. "No dessert?" Ronan asked carefully.

"I was thinking we should go to the grocery store. Stock up for Friday night's cookoff."

"You want to find out my secret ingredients, don't you?" he teased.

She gave an airy shrug.

Ronan paid the bill, and they walked to the truck.

She glanced at her watch. "Maybe we don't have time for shopping. What else should we do?"

Ronan looked at her and was unable to hold back his grin.

She narrowed her eyes. "We're not having sex."

He laughed, then opened the passenger side door of his truck. "I didn't say we were. We can do anything you want." He closed the door, then went around and got into the driver's seat.

Alison grasped his hand. "I'm not trying to send you mixed messages. I just..."

He gave her hand a squeeze. "You don't have to explain. We only met four days ago. I'm capable of being a gentleman."

He found it hard to live up to that promise when Alison slid closer and cupped his face. His heart jumped into overdrive as she pressed her lips against his. She tasted of pizza and root beer. Her soft sigh when he kissed her back nearly drove him crazy, and he wanted like hell to find out what the rest of her tasted like. She broke the kiss.

His slipped his fingers into her hair and whispered in her ear, "Still no?"

She smiled against his cheek, pressed a quick kiss to his lips, then drew back. "Still no. I hate to end this already, but I really should pick up Emmy from my mom."

"I understand. We can take our time, honey," he murmured. "A slow burn."

Alison smiled her thanks, then slid back by the door.

Friday couldn't come soon enough.

CHAPTER TWENTY-FIVE

ALISON WORE A "KISS THE COOK" APRON, BARE FEET, AND the prettiest smile Ronan had ever seen. He liked having her in his house and cooking in his kitchen. He glimpsed a life that could be if he played his cards right, if he didn't push her into a relationship she wasn't ready for. All he had to do was take things slow.

"Having fun?" He slung a towel over his shoulder.

"I've been waiting all week for this," she said. "Who are our judges? Obviously, I'll vote for my chili and you'll vote for yours."

"Kelly Ann and Diego will be here in about hour."

"Your sister and best friend." Alison snorted. "That's not biased at all."

Ronan laughed. "What are you talking about? They love you."

"Mm. What's your secret ingredient?" Alison asked him over her shoulder. She was standing on her toes and scanning the spice rack.

Ronan left his pot on simmer, then walked up behind her and wrapped his arms around her waist. He'd been dying to touch her since her arrival. "I'll tell you mine if you tell me yours."

She laughed as he kissed the crook of her neck. "I don't believe you."

"Liquid smoke," he said.

Alison shook her head. "That's your secret? Isn't that a necessity in all chili recipes?"

He poked her side and groaned when she squirmed against his body.

"Sorry."

"Oh, never apologize for that, Alison."

She turned in his arms and peered up at him. "You're a really nice guy."

He grimaced.

"No, I mean...I enjoy being with you."

"Good. Because I intend to spend a lot more time with you. Don't worry," he added before she could reply, "I know you have a daughter and you're starting college. I'll take anything you're willing to give."

He didn't tell her what he hoped she would give. Or all that he imagined doing to her.

Steam rattled the lid of his chili pot.

"Damn." Ronan released her to face the stovetop and stir his perfect 80:20 ratio of beef and Italian sausage.

Alison stepped up to the stove and lifted the lid on her chili. She picked up the spoon lying on the spoon rest beside the pot. "I didn't mean to distract you."

He turned down the heat and tasted the chili. A dash of cayenne would add just the right amount of zing. "Don't worry about it."

He added the cayenne, then stirred the chili and inhaled the steam rising from the pot. Just about perfect. Ronan set his spoon down and pulled Alison back into his arms. Something about cooking turned him on. Heat, spices, chemistry.

"Hey, I'm cooking." She shook the bottle of red pepper flakes she held.

Ronan looked at the small jar. "Red pepper flakes. Excellent choice."

"Cheater." Alison laughed.

He laughed and kissed her temple. He could get used to her laughter in his kitchen.

"You'll never guess who I ran into at college today," she said against his chest.

"Who?" he asked.

"Kelly Ann."

"Bribing a cookoff judge before the main event, huh?" He hugged her tighter.

Alison's laughter filled his kitchen. "She was excited about coming over here tonight. I honestly had no idea."

"She likes you," Ronan said.

Alison drew back and looked up at him. "How do you know? Not that I'm looking for reassurance."

"Of course not." He ran his fingers through the hair framing her face. "She told me."

"What did she say?" Alison pressed.

"That you're too good for me."

She snorted. "How was the rest of your week? You're back at work, aren't you?"

"I am."

"That's all I get?" she asked.

Her hands that pressed to the small of his back were a distraction, but he was a grown man. He could focus on an adult conversation.

"It was good to be back. Thankfully, there were no fires to

deal with, but we did have a pretty bad car wreck. Had to remove the driver's side door to extricate a woman."

She pulled free of his embrace and turned to her pot of chili. "I heard about that on the news. Was the driver okay?"

"Bruised, but she should be fine."

"Thank God," Alison said. "How do you cope with that?"

"With seeing people on their worst days?" He lifted the lid on his chili and stirred the thick soup. "Honestly, it took some getting used to. When I started with the department, I used to bring a lot home with me. I still harass the fire marshal and police for information on the fires that seem like more than just accidents."

She grinned.

"What?" he asked.

"You're an amateur detective."

Ronan added a shot of Worcestershire sauce to his simmering pot of heaven. "I'm not known for following rules."

"Even your own?"

"Even my own."

"Thank you for tonight. For planning this."

He froze when Alison lifted on her toes and pressed a kiss to his cheek.

He turned his head slightly and looked down at her. "You're so beautiful.'

"Don't distract me with flattery." Her cheeks turned a pretty pink. "I'm determined to win this cookoff."

Ronan kissed her mouth, quick and hard, then lifted both hands. "I'll keep my hands to myself."

"Until I win a kiss, right? That was the prize?" she asked, eyebrow raised.

The doorbell rang before he had a chance to respond.

"Hold that thought. The judges are here." Ronan hurried through the living room and opened the front door. "Hey." He forced a smile. One day he would get used to the way Diego's arm casually draped his baby sister's shoulders.

He glanced past them at the snow. At least three inches had fallen since Alison's arrival. He stepped aside. "Come on in. How bad is it out there?"

"It's really picking up." Diego stood aside and let Kelly Ann enter first. "I thought the blizzard was forecasted for tomorrow."

"It smells great in here." Kelly Ann wrapped her arms around Ronan's waist "Where's Alison?"

Ronan jabbed a thumb over his shoulder. "The kitchen."

She hurried away and left Ronan facing his buddy.

"Nothing's happened between Kelly Ann and me. Yet," Diego said. "So, relax."

Ronan shook his head. The word *yet* was sure to drive him crazy.

They went to the kitchen. Kelly Ann stood over Ronan's pot of chili, lid in hand, and took a deep breath.

"This smells great." She glanced at Ronan then replaced the lid.

Alison shot him an I-told-you-so look and he grinned.

Diego helped himself to a beer from Ronan's fridge.

"Out of the kitchen." Ronan gave his sister a gentle shove. "This could be considered cheating."

"I'm not cheating. It all smells great to me."

"Come on, babe." Diego grasped her hand and pulled her toward the living room. Kelly Ann laughed as she dropped onto the couch beside Diego and changed the television channel from a football game to a chick flick.

Ronan stepped up behind Alison. "Yours smells amazing."

"You don't have to butter me up because I'm the company," she said.

"I'm doing no such thing. You're the competition." Ronan placed a kiss on her shoulder then stepped sideways and lifted the lid on his chili. As good as his chili smelled, he had serious competition.

"Ready?" he asked.

"As ready as I'll ever be."

Ronan pulled three white and three red bowls from the cabinet. She waited patiently as he filled the white bowls with his chili and set them on the table.

Ronan glanced at her. "You know this is just for fun, right?" he said. "You're looking pretty serious."

"I know," she said. "But I'm trying to impress you."

Her cheeks pinked, and his cock jerked. Damn, she was beautiful.

"Just me?" he asked.

"Just you."

"What if I told you I was already impressed?" Ronan tucked a lock of her dark hair behind her ear. "It's only been a week since you were rescued from a burning building, and you've just competed in your first chili cookoff."

"So, if I lose, I have an excuse?" Alison bit her lip.

"There are no losers," he said. "I'm going to kiss you no matter what. You might remember that my kisses are quite a prize."

Alison looked at him from beneath her lashes. "I might need reminding."

Ronan leaned close, then stopped, his mouth a hair's breadth from hers. "Chili first?"

"Oh, no you don't." Alison grasped the back of his head and held him close. "I need an appetizer."

Their mouths touched. Ronan tugged her closer and traced her bottom lip with his tongue. When her tongue made contact with his, he groaned, and slipped his tongue inside her mouth. She tasted like tomato sauce and sweetness. His cock hardened. God, he wanted her.

"Is the chili rea—?" Kelly Ann broke off as Alison jerked back. His sister lifted her hands and backed up two paces. "Whoa, never mind."

Ronan sighed and released Alison. "Take two bowls of chili into the dining room, Kel. We'll bring the other four."

Alison faced the stove, clearly trying to hide her blush, and picked up one of the red bowls on the counter.

Ronan crossed his arms and leaned against the pantry. He couldn't stop smiling. "Kel. Out."

She giggled, picked up two bowls of chili, turned, and called, as she breezed out the kitchen door, "Sorry for the interruption."

"I like her." Alison set the first full bowl on the counter, picked up an empty bowl, and began filling it.

"Yeah, we all wish we could harness her energy sometimes." Ronan pulled six spoons from the silverware drawer. "Don't be embarrassed, Alison."

"I want her to like me. I don't want anyone to think I'm..."

"No one thinks you're anything but fabulous. Including me." He winked. "Especially me."

He handed her the spoons, then picked up two bowls of chili. "Let's go."

They went to the dining room and Ronan set the bowls on the table. Alison put a spoon in each bowl then looked at his sister and Diego.

"Okay," Ronan said. "Vote red or white as your favorite. Bonus points if you can guess who made which batch of chili."

Kelly Ann tried Ronan's first. She chewed thoughtfully, then tried Alison's. "They're both delicious. The chili in the red bowl is sweet, delicious, and rich. Full of body. The chili in the white bowl is hot and spicy. It burns even after you've swallowed. Kind of tangy, too."

"You're quite the chili connoisseur, Miss McGuire," Diego said with a grin. "I'm impressed."

"Ronan has been spoiling us with his cooking for the last couple years. I've become an expert taster." She laughed. "In fact, he's been working away in the kitchen for years. I think Grams has photos of him in her pink, frilly apron."

"Oh, I'm going to need to see those," Diego said.

"Me, too." Alison flashed a sweet smile.

Ronan groaned. "Or not."

"Well, I vote for the white bowl." Kelly Ann dropped her spoon in her now-empty bowl.

"Me, too," Diego said.

Alison picked up one of the spare spoons, scooped a level spoonful from the white bowl, and ate. She nodded slowly. "And me."

Ronan picked up the last spoon and tried Alison's chili. "I like the red." He meant it. Alison had talent in the kitchen. Her chili was damn good.

"So..." Diego looked at Ronan. "The white is yours?"

"Yes."

"You're not gloating?" Kelly Ann asked. "I'm surprised."

Alison laughed. "Is he usually a sore winner?"

"He has his moments," his sister said.

Alison extended a hand toward Ronan. He grasped her hand and gently squeezed.

"A well won competition," she murmured. "Your chili is divine."

"Thank you." He yanked her to him and gave her a sound kiss.

She blinked up at him in surprise when he released her.

Ronan lifted a brow. "I told you, win or lose, I would kiss you."

Alison shook her head in a mock reprimand, but he read the pleasure in her eyes.

His cell phone rang. Ronan crossed to the counter between the dining room and kitchen and grabbed the phone. Keith's name flashed on the screen.

His boss was calling on a Friday night?

This couldn't be good.

CHAPTER TWENTY-SIX

SNOW FELL IN HUGE, THICK FLAKES WHEN RONAN STEPPED onto the front porch. He closed the door behind him before answering his cell.

"What's the good word, Lieutenant?"

"Nothing good to report, McGuire."

Ronan tensed. "What's going on, sir?"

"O'Malley finished her investigation of the fire at Andie's. Of course, like you said, gasoline. I guess Janis spoke with you, and she handed over the name Jenson Williams to the police as a possible suspect. After flunking out of fire training, he worked for J&M Demolition, which—"

"Is owned by the guy whose garage burned down last week," Ronan finished for him.

"Right," Keith said. "The cops aren't sure if he torched the bar because half our department was there or if someone from J&M happened to be there."

"Fuck," Ronan muttered.

"I know."

Ronan didn't like the grim note in his boss's voice. "Is there something else?"

A beat of silence passed, then Keith said, "Williams is missing."

"Fuck," Ronan said again. "This doesn't make sense. The other fires had nothing to do with the Rapid Falls Fire Department. Why's he suddenly coming after us?"

"Based on what the detective told me, I'd say he set the fires because he likes to watch them burn. Well, aside from this garage fire last week. Seems he and his boss had a falling out. That was pure revenge."

"Andie's was pure revenge, too," Ronan said. "For not making the squad?"

"Maybe."

Ronan released a breath. "Thanks for the heads up. Diego's here. I'll give him the news."

"No dating in the firehouse, McGuire."

"He's seeing Kelly Ann."

"Yeah, I know," Keith said. "How are you taking that?"

"Not as well as finding out that some asshole is trying to burn employees of the Rapid Falls Fire Department alive."

"Go easy on Diego. He's a good man."

"I know." The front door opened and Ronan looked over his shoulder as Diego stepped outside. "Call me if there are any updates." Ronan ended the call.

"Everything okay?" Diego leaned against the railing, looking all too comfortable in Ronan's world.

"We think the arsonist who hit the bar was the same punk who set that garage on fire last week."

Diego straightened from the railing. "Well, fuck."

"Yeah. Keith said to watch our backs," Ronan said. "Listen, Diego. Janis and I were talking last week at Andie's. Do you remember Jenson Williams? He attended a couple of training courses we took about a year ago."

Diego frowned. "Big guy? A little squirrelly?" He gave a slow nod. "Yeah. He drank with us one night."

"You went drinking with him?" Ronan asked in surprise.

"Threw back at least ten beers," Diego said. "What kind was it, again? Said he only drank that kind. Got lucky whenever he did." Diego snapped his fingers. "*Red Cap*."

"*Red Cap*?" Ronan blurted.

Diego regarded him. "Yeah, why?"

"There was a *Red Cap* bottle cap at the garage fire."

"Jesus," Diego muttered. "He's gotta be the guy. Maybe you should tell Janis."

Ronan tapped the screen on his phone and pulled up Janis's number. The call went to voicemail. He left a message and told her to call back when she got the chance.

"Should you call the cops and give them the information?" Diego asked. "They need to be looking for this guy."

"They are," Ronan said. "He's missing."

"You're fucking kidding me," Diego said.

Ronan shook his head. "I wish I was."

"Jesus, let's hope that means he doesn't have time to set anymore fires."

Ronan nodded. He surveyed the street. No asphalt was visible beneath the inches of glistening snow. "I'm thinking you and Kelly Ann will be staying here tonight." As would Alison.

Diego nodded, then turned and crossed his arms over his chest. "Listen, McGuire. I appreciate you being cool with me and Kelly Ann."

Ronan rubbed the back his neck. "No one said anything about being cool."

Diego laughed. "She's a great girl. You should be proud of her."

"I'm damn proud of her."

"What had you freaked out at your grandma's house?"

Diego laughed. "I noticed a lot of dirty looks thrown my direction. We were good on New Year's Eve, weren't we?"

"To be honest, watching my sister with Alison's baby had me a little rattled. It made it real. She's grown up."

Diego laughed again. "You think that scared you? I damn near pissed myself."

"We're on the same page then?" Ronan asked.

"Damn straight."

The door opened and Kelly Ann peeked out. "We need to go, Diego. I just saw on the news that driving conditions are getting pretty bad."

"I think you should stay," Ronan said.

Kelly Ann's eyes brightened, then she waggled her brows. "Sleep over."

CHAPTER TWENTY-SEVEN

At half past one, Ronan entered the small bedroom that he had converted into a den.

Alison looked up from the news. "Is everyone all tucked in?"

"Diego is set up on the sofa, and Kelly Ann is in my spare room behind squeaky door hinges."

"That's a bit evil, isn't it?" Alison asked as he lowered himself onto the couch beside her.

He wrapped an arm around her and pulled her close. "I never said I was a good guy."

"Promises, promises."

His wink was anything but angelic. "Oh, before I forget." He picked up a wrapped gift with a bow on top sitting on the coffee table. "I have something for you."

The large square gift was clearly some type of book, but she said, "How did you have time to run to Tiffany's?"

"Well, this is going to be a letdown compared to jewelry." He gave her the present. "But I hope you like it."

"Is this my consolation prize for losing the cookoff?" she asked.

Ronan laughed and kissed her cheek. "Your chili was amazing. I voted for yours."

"A pity vote. Everyone else chose yours. Even me," Alison admitted. "I saw the ancho chilis you put in yours."

He nodded. "They add depth of flavor. There's no way Jerry is going to win this year."

Alison snorted. "Okay, that's sexy."

His brows rose. "My ingredients or my competitive nature?"

"Both," she said.

"I'm glad you think so. I'd like to cook for you again sometime." He tapped the gift she still held. "But for now, open the gift."

She laughed at his childlike excitement as she tore at the Christmas wrap to reveal the Rapid Falls Firefighter Charity Calendar. She was such an idiot. She should've known.

He winked. "Don't have one, do you?"

"Now that you mention it, I feel bad I didn't think to buy one," she said.

"Don't feel bad. That wasn't the point. Open it up to July."

She flipped through the pages, past the guys posing shirtless in front of the firetruck, in front of a hydrant spraying water, and even Trevor with a dalmatian puppy in his arms.

Then she reached July. Ronan stood in front of a flaming building, shirtless, sweat dewy on his softly hairy chest, holding his bright yellow helmet in his left hand. He had a grin on his face, not cocky, as if someone had made him laugh before taking the picture.

"Oh, my God. That is one sexy photo, Ronan."

"You really haven't seen it?" he asked.

"I was too busy trying to avoid you." Alison ran her fingers across his broad shoulders and read aloud the message written in felt pen, "Alison, If you ever get too hot, give me a call. Yours, Ronan."

"Well?" He looked shy again, as if her opinion really mattered to him.

She held his gaze. "What if I'm hot now?"

He kissed her, slow and sweet, then murmured against her mouth, "Mr. July is at your service."

"I'm a lucky girl." She patted his chest and warmth rippled through her. The man was pure steel.

"I live to serve."

Alison blew out a deep breath. "That's sexy, too."

"Should I get my helmet?"

God, if he put on his helmet, she wouldn't be able to resist. Could she resist now?

"A little TV?" he asked. "Or would you prefer to go to bed?"

She frowned. "I can't put you out of your bed. This couch will do for me."

He shook his head. "No way."

Alison sighed. He'd already refused three times to let her sleep on the couch. "We can share the couch."

He snatched the remote from the coffee table and changed the channel as he pulled her against his shoulder. "I'll take anything you want to give, baby."

An action film filled the thirty-six-inch TV screen. Ronan turned down the volume. "Any requests?"

Alison shook her head and relaxed against him. He was so warm and solid. She missed Emmy, but hated to think of morning, when she would have to leave him.

"I forgot to ask earlier, how are Joey and Megan doing with the bar?" Ronan squeezed her shoulder.

"They've gotten three good estimates on the repairs. They're waiting to hear back from the insurance company."

"God, how long will that take?"

She shook her head. "I don't know. Megan isn't one to be

patient about stuff like this. She'll bug them until they make a decision."

"Good for her."

"I have a job interview lined up for a sports bar close to campus, just until Andie's reopens."

Ronan pressed his lips to her temple. "You're amazing."

Alison closed her eyes and snuggled closer to Ronan. With the hand around her shoulder, he pulled an afghan from the back of the couch down onto her.

"Comfy?" he asked.

She nodded. This was heaven. Levi hadn't been one for cuddling. He was more a six-minute man. Five minutes of sex, then asleep in sixty seconds. She didn't think it possible to fall asleep in sixty seconds with this man beside her. She might not be able to sleep at all. What if Ronan didn't feel the same way? He clearly wanted to have sex with her, but that didn't mean he would be any different than Levi.

No, Ronan *was* different. But what if Levi hadn't just been an asshole? What if she wasn't interesting?

Alison tried focusing on the TV, but all she could envision was Ronan getting up from the bed and sneaking from the room while he thought she slept. Which was stupid. He wouldn't sneak out of his own house and leave her there. Would he be disappointed, though?

"Alison?"

She started, tilted her head back, and looked up at him.

"You okay?"

She nodded, unable to speak.

His brow furrowed.

"You really don't have to give up your bed," she said.

He frowned, and Alison winced inwardly. She was a complete idiot.

"You said we could share the couch. Right?"

She nodded. A gleam entered his eyes, and her heart skipped a beat as his mouth lowered onto hers. Alison wrapped her arms around his neck. He tugged the afghan aside, pulled her up farther on the cushion, then came down on top of her. The hard planes of his body felt as good as she'd known they would.

He flicked his tongue against her mouth, then whispered, "You taste wonderful," in the instant before his tongue slipped inside her mouth.

His tongue tangled with hers, sending a message straight to the throb between her legs. Alison speared her hands into the downy hair at the nape of his neck. God, it felt like forever since she'd been touched by a man.

Ronan growled and slipped a hand beneath her shirt. He flattened a palm on her ribs and slid his hand upward. Her nipple hardened almost painfully in anticipation of his warm hand on her breast.

He broke the kiss and whispered in her ear, "You okay with this, baby?"

Her head whirled. She was more than okay. She wanted him so badly it hurt.

"I don't want you to regret anything tomorrow," she murmured.

He blinked. "Me? Regret anything? Fuck, I'll show you what I'm thinking."

He rose, and her heart took a dive. He didn't want her after all.

He scooped her into his arms so unexpectedly that she cried out.

"Ronan, what are you doing?"

He grinned. "I'm going to show you how much I want you."

Ronan strode from the den and into his bedroom. He shoved the door closed with his hip, then took two steps to the bed and dropped onto the mattress, landing on top of her. He cut off her laugh with a kiss that stole her breath.

Heat flashed through her when he thrust his hard length against her abdomen. Her head whirled. Was it wrong to want him this badly? It had been so long—not just since a man had touched her, but since a man had really made love to her. She didn't know Ronan well enough to think of that word—love— but it fit this moment. It fit what she wanted him to do to her. Dare she hope that he felt the same?

He broke the kiss and sat up. Alison drew a breath when he pulled his shirt up over his head. Ronan was the living image of every woman's fantasy: shirtless, hard, perfect muscles, pierced nipples, that sexy shoulder tattoo. What woman could resist a bad boy with a heart of gold?

He lifted his brows. "Like what you see?"

Alison met his gaze "You need to take off your jeans."

"Yes, ma'am." He jumped to his feet and shoved his jeans down so fast Alison could barely contain a laugh.

He crossed his arms over his chest and her insides melted. "Your turn," he said.

Her turn? Oh, God. She steeled her nerves, sat up, and pulled her shirt over her head. Alison tried not to think about her breasts nearly spilling out over her lacy bra. She wasn't making milk like she used to, but her breasts were still larger than they used to be.

Ronan waited. Alison unbuttoned her jeans, then lowered the zipper and shimmied them down her legs. His eyes darkened and she resisted an urge to pull the covers over herself.

"My turn again?" he whispered, and she realized he was asking permission to strip naked.

Her heartbeat sped up. She gave a small nod.

Ronan pushed his boxer briefs down his hips, and her mouth went dry at sight of his thick erection. The guy was built to please. Then she saw the curved piece of steel through the head of his cock.

"Is that…?"

He laughed. "Oh, it is."

Her heart jumped into overdrive, as he climbed into bed beside her. His warm mouth covered hers, and he pressed his body close. His cock dug into her belly and made her head spin.

Alison threw one leg over his hip and gasped when his hand slipped beneath her panties and between her legs.

Ronan froze. "Not good?"

"Too good."

He smiled, then nipped her earlobe as he gently slid a finger inside her. "We can stop if it's too much or too soon."

"I don't know if it's fair to say that when your finger is inside me."

Ronan buried his face in her shoulder and laughed. Alison shoved him back, closed her lips around his nipple and flicked that little gold ring with her tongue.

"Fuck me," he breathed.

"I was planning on it, actually," she said, and basked in his laughter. She hated serious sex.

"Yeah? I like that plan." He nudged her legs wider with his knee.

"Is this going to be the *Quick Fuck* you offered me last week?"

His smile stole her breath. All the shyness she'd seen when he stood shirtless on the stage had vanished. "I lied. I don't do quick."

Her breath whooshed from her lungs as he trailed kisses down her belly and tugged down her panties. As his mouth made contact with her moist folds, he slid from the bed.

God, it had been so long, she was going to orgasm that instant.

"Ronan," she breathed. Need tightened her stomach.

He pulled her panties off her feet and slipped a finger inside her again. Pleasure rippled through her. Ronan nipped at her clit, then flicked his tongue against the sensitive nub. When he closed his mouth over her and sucked, she arched against his tongue. Her orgasm rose with startling speed and intensity. Alison cried out and fisted the blanket.

"Ronan."

He sucked harder.

Another orgasm tightened her clit, and she bowed off the bed. Pleasure ripped through her, and she was sure her eyes rolled back in her head.

Slowly, he pressed kisses to her inner thighs and she relaxed against the mattress. His promise of taking his time, combined with the French kissing between her legs, made her pray he had told the truth. Alison never wanted this moment to end.

"I'll pay you five hundred dollars to do that again," her words were breathy, but she couldn't find it in herself to be embarrassed. Those had been the greatest orgasms of her life.

He chuckled and kissed the beauty mark on her inner thigh. "I work for free, Alison. Not allowed to take gifts, remember?"

Then his tongue flicked her swollen sex again and she couldn't remember her name. His fingers dug into her thighs as he kept them open wide. Her body shook with delightful tremor after tremor. The man's mouth was magic.

"Was I too loud?" she asked after she caught her breath.

He grinned. "The walls are thin around here, but I think everyone's asleep. Don't worry about it."

"You're lying, but I don't care. God, Ronan."

"I think I like you melty and soft," Ronan whispered as he crawled back onto the bed.

"You don't miss my smart mouth?"

He squeezed her breasts over her bra. "Your mouth is about

to be far too busy for talking," he teased. He winked and flexed his pecs, making his little gold hoops dance.

"Is that so?"

Next to her, the mattress sank under his body weight and she rolled against his warm body.

He comforted her by wrapping his arms around her. "I want you, Alison."

She cupped his face and rubbed her thumbs over his five o'clock shadow. "Levi made me believe I didn't deserve this."

"A crazy firefighter?" He grinned. "Everyone deserves one of those." His expression sobered. "You're beautiful when you smile." He bumped her nose with his. "You want me on top?"

"I want you inside me. How you manage to do that is up to you."

He reached into the nightstand for a condom and rolled it on. He rolled on top of her, fitted his cock to her opening, and pushed into her. "Now, see. I did miss the smart mouth."

"Dear God, Ronan."

He sucked at her pulse point while he thrust into her—hard. All her mind could focus on was the friction between her legs, the fire in her belly, and that piercing that rubbed just the right place.

"Faster? Slower?" he said, voice hoarse. "Tell me how you like it."

"Make me come. Right now."

He met her gaze, eyes intense. "That's my girl."

Ronan gently eased her legs up to her chest and slowly thrust into her. She couldn't believe how much bigger he felt this way, as if he touched all of her at once. He plunged into her faster and faster. A few hard thrusts, and her climax rolled over her with an intensity that caused her body to bow. He tugged her bra down and buried his face between her breasts as he thrust harder. When he groaned with his own release, another climax rolled over her, and it felt as if her soul shattered.

At last, she drew a much-needed breath. "I think that was the best sex of my life."

He pulled out and had the audacity to tickle her throbbing clit. She came again with a scream she feared would wake the household.

He gave her another kiss and grinned. "You think?"

She shook her head, breathing heavily. "I'm certain. I'll never walk again."

"You're welcome."

"You're so arrogant." Alison barely recognized her own breathy voice.

"In a good way?"

She threw her arms over her head and sighed as she watched him walk to the en suite bathroom. "You're entitled to be, that's for sure."

He returned a moment later, a cocky grin on his face. "I never want to stop hearing that sound."

"My embarrassingly loud screams?" she asked.

"It makes me hard just thinking about it."

He dropped onto the mattress and took one of her bare feet in his hands and sucked her toe. Alison howled with laughter and tried to twist free, but he held fast. She grabbed a pillow and swatted him with it.

He ducked and released her foot, then jumped on her. "Oh, you're in for it now."

"Yeah?" she asked, her eyes locked with his. "Bring it on."

CHAPTER TWENTY-EIGHT

Ronan met Alison's shining eyes in the mirror over the bathroom sink. He never would have thought brushing his teeth beside a beautiful, naked woman would be so damn satisfying.

"What?" she asked, looking shy and sexy at once. Her hair was a tousled mess, her eyes were wide, and she had a speck of toothpaste on the corner of her mouth.

Ronan wiped the froth from his mouth with a fluffy white face towel and then from hers. "You're beautiful."

She turned to face him and stared at his naked body, pausing to get a better look at the crest and flames on his shoulder, and finally returned the smile. "Ditto."

"You don't seem like the kind of girl who would be into tatts and piercings," he said.

"Why?" she asked. "Because I'm a mom?"

"Because, behind that smart mouth of yours, you're sweet as spun sugar."

"Oh. Cotton candy." She swished her mouth with water, then rubbed her thumb over her full bottom lip. "I'm hungry."

Ronan pulled her into his arms and kissed her. "Alison."

Her cheeks flushed when he met her eyes. "Yes?"

"I want you to know that this, us, it's important to me. I want more than a one-night stand."

Her expression turned serious. "Good."

"You're not sick of me yet?" he asked.

She shook her head.

"Even though I'm arrogant?"

"Especially because you're arrogant."

"I'm not though. Just in bed."

Alison rolled her eyes. "Sure thing, Mr. July."

He growled and pulled her against his body. His cock hardened when she shivered.

"What are you thinking?" her question was soft, and he detected uncertainty.

Ronan hugged her close. "You're fucking gorgeous." He kissed her collarbone.

"Where have you been the last ten months?" she teased.

"Eating chili. Learning how to cook better chili."

"Chili turns you on, does it?" she asked.

"Well, you *have* tasted my chili."

"Gets all the girls wet, does it?"

His eyes darkened. "Let's find out."

He walked her backwards until she bumped into the closed bathroom door. He wanted to touch her all over—slowly. Ronan kissed her, tangling his tongue with hers, and need ripped through him.

Her breath hitched. "I'm not going anywhere, Ronan."

"Doesn't matter," he said against her mouth. "I can't get enough of you."

He kissed her until she moaned.

"Get a condom. *Now*," she ordered.

Ronan broke the embrace and managed to make it to the

medicine cabinet. He pulled a condom from the box there and faced her.

"How many boxes of those do you have?" Alison asked. "One in every room?"

He grinned. "Possibly. It makes sense, huh?"

"I can't argue with that logic."

She dropped to her knees, but instead of opening the package, she wrapped slim fingers around his cock. Ronan braced his arms against the door and watched as she closed her full lips over the head of his erection.

She used the tip of her tongue to toy with his piercing and he thanked his lucky damn stars he had decided on his Prince Albert. Pleasure tightened his balls. God, she was sexy as hell with her lips around his cock. He was going to come in her mouth.

Ronan grasped her shoulders and pulled back. He couldn't repress a groan as she slid her lips over his cock the instant before he sprang free.

She snapped her head up and frowned. "Did I do something wrong?"

He gave a hoarse laugh and dragged her up into a hug. "Baby, all you have to do is look at me and I'm hard as a rock."

Ronan froze when her tongue made contact with his nipple. He didn't dare move as she flattened a hand on his chest until a finger slipped into his left nipple ring and tugged. He closed his eyes and willed his lust into submission. If he came against her belly, she would think he was no better than a sixteen-year-old.

"I need you," she whispered.

Thank God.

"Yes, ma'am."

Ronan took the condom from her, rolled it on, then cupped her ass and lifted her. She wrapped her legs around his hips, and he carried her back into the bedroom. He took one step toward the bed, then turned right and backed her against the wall. She laughed, then kissed him hard when he crushed her between the wall and his body.

Ronan fitted his erection to her opening. She buried her head in his shoulder as he thrust inside her. Fuck, he had never felt such a powerful, torrid attraction to a woman.

THE SQUEAK of Kelly Ann's bedroom door jarred Ronan awake.

Alison stirred in his arms. "Everything okay?"

Ronan pressed a kiss to the top of her head. "Everything's great." So long as Kelly Ann wasn't sneaking out to join Diego on the sofa.

Ronan rolled from bed, pulled on a pair of basketball shorts, and slipped from the room into the hallway. Kelly Ann stood outside the guest bedroom, eyes wide, a blanket wrapped around her. She looked so young without makeup. He could see her freckles even in the dim light of the frosted overhead light, and her hair fell in a long braid over her shoulder.

"I heard something," she whispered. "The back gate squeaked. I didn't open the curtains."

"Come on." He grasped her arm and guided her the half dozen steps to his room. They reached the door as the nightstand light lit the room. Ronan halted just outside the door and looked inside the room. Alison sat on the edge of the bed, dressed in his t-shirt and her jeans.

"What's wrong?" she asked.

He urged his sister into the room. "Kelly Ann heard a noise. I'm going to check it out."

"What about Diego?" Kelly Ann said. "We can't leave him alone."

As if Diego, the master of the bench press, needed his protection. "Diego will come with me. Go." Ronan gently pushed her toward Alison.

Alison's brow furrowed in worry. "Maybe we should call the police."

"It's probably nothing." Ronan smiled. "Diego and I will be back in a jiff."

He reached the living room to find the side table lamp on and Diego getting to his feet. "What's going on?" Diego asked.

"Kelly Ann heard a noise out back. I figured we could take a look."

Ronan glimpsed the flicker in Diego's eyes and knew he was thinking the same thing Ronan was: how likely was it that Williams had tracked Ronan down?

CHAPTER TWENTY-NINE

Kelly Ann didn't seem surprised to find Alison in Ronan's bed, but Alison was thankful she'd dressed. Little sister was more grown up than Ronan realized.

Kelly Ann sat beside Alison at the foot of Ronan's bed and took her hand.

"What did you hear?" Alison asked.

"Footsteps."

"You sure it was footsteps?" she asked.

"Yes. It was the crunch of snow." With her eyes wide, Kelly Ann looked so young and innocent.

A tremor of fear rippled through Alison, but she gave Kelly Ann a reassuring smile.

"It was probably a dog. The guys will be all right."

She swallowed. "I overheard him talking to Diego on the porch. There's some guy on the loose who's targeting members of the fire department."

"What?" Alison blurted before catching herself. "That can't be right," she quickly amended, but thought of the fire at Andie's.

"It's true," Kelly Ann said. "This is as bad as worrying every time he goes in for a shift."

"He's a tough guy," Alison said. It was so much easier to reassure someone else. Alison knew she wouldn't be so blasé the next time Ronan went to work. "Very brave. A real superhero."

Kelly Ann nodded. "He always has been."

"What was it like growing up with Ronan?" Alison asked. She had to admit to some curiosity, but, more than anything, she wanted to distract Kelly Ann.

"Ronan is eight years older than me, so he's always looked out for me. I can't think of a better person than my brother. He's sweet and selfless, and he loves Granny and me so much that Granny had to practically throw him out of the house after he graduated college."

"He's a protector," Alison said. "It's in his nature, isn't it?"

It warmed Alison's heart to hear his sister validate her impression of Ronan. Her wildly accelerated relationship with him seemed so right already. "He really seems like a nice guy." She winced inwardly at how silly she sounded. She was, after all, in the man's bedroom.

Kelly Ann laughed. "Ronan doesn't have secrets. He is exactly who he seems to be."

Alison gave a look of mock sternness. "How much is he paying you?"

Kelly Ann gave her a shy smile. "Maybe I want to keep you, too."

Alison started at the longing that rippled through her. "I've never had a sister."

"Did you hear shouting?" Kelly Ann jumped up and ran to the window.

Alison's pulse accelerated. Ronan couldn't really be in trouble, could he?

CHAPTER THIRTY

Ronan zipped up his coat as he and Diego stepped out onto the porch. The snow had finally stopped and glistened pristine and untouched in the moonlight.

"You know the smart thing would be to call the police," Diego said.

"If there is an intruder, he'll be gone before the police get here." Ronan turned on his flashlight.

"What did Kelly Ann hear exactly?" Diego asked.

"The gate latch that opens into the alley. It's the only gate out back." Ronan slid the flashlight beam across the front yard.

"Backyard?" Diego asked.

Ronan nodded and descended the three steps into calf-high snow with Diego close behind. They trudged through the snow around the side of the house, then halted while Ronan swept the beam across the backyard. He stopped the beam on footprints that had led from the back gate to the right side of the house and back to the fence.

"Fuck," Ronan cursed.

"There." Diego pointed to a figure in the alley.

The figure stood six and a half feet tall, shoulders like a tank.

Jenson Williams.

Williams turned, vaulted the neighbor's fence, and dropped out of sight into Becket's yard.

Rage shot through Ronan. He would end this bullshit tonight. He and Diego took off at a run. They reached the neighbor's fence in three long bounds and both vaulted over and into deep snow on the other side. Ronan ran the flashlight beam over the ground. His blood went cold when the footsteps ended two feet away, then turned—

Something hard connected with the side of Ronan's head. He stumbled forward, dropping the flashlight. The light disappeared in the snow. Diego shouted a curse, and Ronan glimpsed a blur as the two men rolled in the snow.

Ronan shook his head in an effort to clear his vision. The sharp odor of gasoline burned his nostrils. The two men crashed into Ronan's legs. He stumbled backward and fell, ass first, in the snow. One of the fighters landed a punch to the other's jaw. Ronan couldn't tell who was who. He shoved to his feet. Pain shot down his neck and his vision blurred.

A light in the corner of Ronan's eye caught his attention.

"Fuck," Diego growled.

Ronan turned to see Williams get to his feet and tower over him. Ronan rammed into him shoulder first. They hit the ground, Ronan landing on top of Williams. His head bounced off Williams' chest. Pain splintered down his neck, and Williams rammed a fist into his ribs.

Ronan pushed off and rolled out of his reach, then pushed onto his knees. Williams started to rise. Diego leapt, landed beside Williams, and kicked him in the ribs. The man growled and grabbed for Diego's ankle. Diego cursed and jumped out of reach.

Ronan brought the heel of his shoe down on the side of Williams' head. Williams cried out. Diego rammed a fist into the big man's face. Williams went limp.

"You okay?" Diego panted.

Ronan stared at Williams though blurry eyes.

"Ronan," Diego called.

Ronan jerked his gaze onto Diego.

"You okay?" Diego asked.

Ronan squinted at Diego. His head pounded.

"What the hell?" Diego cursed. "The house is on fire."

"What?" Ronan blurted. Understanding struck as he whirled. Firelight lit the night—and his house.

Kelly Ann and Alison.

Ronan vaulted the fence without a second thought or hesitation. Diego dropped to the ground beside him. Fear shot through Ronan at sight of the flames on the side of the house. They sprinted the few paces across the alley, jumped the fence, and raced forward the blaze.

"Fire extinguisher's in the back of my truck," Ronan shouted.

Diego veered right and disappeared around the side of the house. A gas can lay on its side five feet from the flames that now engulfed half the side of the house. He had to get Kelly Ann and Alison out.

Ronan scooped up the gas can and continued at a run around the house. His heart beat faster at the sight of two figures standing on the curb.

Kelly Ann and Alison. He dropped the gas can the second he reached them and dragged them both into his arms.

"What happened?" Kelly Ann asked against his chest, her voice catching.

Ronan forced himself to release them. "I'll explain later."

He met Alison's gaze. The streetlight illuminated her face, and he read fear in her eyes. "You two all right?" He glanced at Kelly Ann, then looked back at Alison.

She nodded. "We called the fire department."

God, she was amazing.

His neighbor across the street burst from his house. "Everyone safe?" John shouted across his yard as he raced toward them.

"Yeah," Ronan shouted back.

John jogged up beside Ronan. "What happened?"

"Don't know yet," Ronan said. He couldn't let the women know an arsonist was on the loose.

"Maybe it's the same guy who set the fire at Andie's," Kelly Ann said.

Ronan blinked. Fuck, how did she know? He caught sight of Diego with the fire extinguisher. More neighbors emerged from their houses.

"You two stay here," Ronan ordered. "Diego and I will do what we can until the firetruck gets here."

Alison nodded and put her arm around Kelly Ann. Ronan cast a glance at John, who nodded in understanding that he would keep an eye on the women, then Ronan hurried back to the fire. Diego had emptied the fire extinguisher on the flames.

"Didn't do much good," Diego said, breathing heavily.

"No." Ronan ran around the house to the small shed and grabbed the shovels stored there. He raced back to Diego and gave him a shovel. They began shoveling snow onto the fire.

Ronan knew only minutes passed, but time seemed to slow to a crawl until a siren sounded in the distance. When the firetruck arrived, he and Diego had stopped the fire from spreading beyond the house. In less than a minute, the fire crew had the hose aimed at the fire.

Ronan left the fire in the capable hands of Firehouse 4 and headed back across the yard toward the alley. Fury pumped through his veins. He would kill Williams. He ran to his neighbor's fence.

"Hey!"

Ronan jerked his head around at Diego's shout. Diego ran toward him.

Ronan jumped the fence. His gut tightened at sight of Williams lying motionless in the snow. Ronan reached him a heartbeat later and seized the big man's collar. Ronan drew back a fist. Fingers of iron closed around his wrist. Ronan snapped his head around to face Diego.

"Can't do it, man," Diego said

"He tried to kill Kelly Ann and Alison," Ronan snarled.

"Yeah," Diego replied, and Ronan was sure he heard barely repressed rage in his friend's voice. "But he should be the only one going to jail tonight."

Ronan hesitated.

"Don't you think I want to kill him, too?" Diego said in a low voice. "But we *have* to be smart about this. We don't want those two women to be left without our protection, do we?"

"Our protection?" Ronan echoed.

Diego released him. "You know if you start beating him, I'll help."

Ronan stared at his friend. "That's stupid."

"No one ever said I was smart."

Williams groaned.

Ronan looked at the man. "We need to tie him up. There's twine in my backyard shed."

Diego didn't move.

Ronan shifted his gaze to him. "I won't hit him."

Still, Diego didn't move.

"I won't kick him, either."

Diego nodded and jumped the fence. Ronan stood alone and bowcord tense beside the man who had tried to kill his sister and the woman he'd fallen in love with.

CHAPTER THIRTY-ONE

RONAN SHIFTED IN THE CHAIR THAT FACED THE DESK OF the officer taking his statement. The side of his head throbbed where Williams had punched him, and he could barely think amid the noise in the police station.

The police had finished taking Kelly Ann's and Alison's statements an hour ago, and Diego's fifteen minutes ago. Ronan had sent them to his Granny's place. Now, he wanted to get out of here to be with Alison. He checked his phone. No messages. Two fires in one week were too many for her—or anyone—to deal with.

She hadn't smiled when she left, hadn't so much as waved. Gut deep dread hurt more than his head. She wasn't going to stick around. He needed to talk to her, but he was stuck here because of Williams.

"Okay, Mr. McGuire," the officer said with as much enthusiasm as expected at three in the morning. He tapped a few more keys on his computer. "I'll print out your statement, then you can sign and be on your way."

"Thank you," Ronan said.

"Hey, McGuire."

Ronan leapt to his feet and whirled at Williams' taunt. Williams struggled against the two officers who were leading him across the room.

"Think you're the shit, huh, McGuire?" Jenson yanked his cuffed arm loose from one officer's grasp.

Ronan started toward the asshole, but the officer taking his statement leapt to his feet and stepped in Ronan's path. "Sit down, sir."

A corner of Williams' mouth twisted upward in a half snarl. "Not so hot after all, are you? How's that pretty girl of yours?"

Ronan charged. The police officer rammed him with a shoulder. Ronan stumbled sideways as blood roared in his ears. He could kill Williams.

Slim fingers closed around Ronan's bicep. He spun to find Janis standing there.

She motioned with her head. "Come on, McGuire."

Fury coursed through his veins.

"*Now,*" she ordered.

He released a breath and followed Officer Janis Rylands into a small room—an interrogation room. She leaned a hip against the steel table in the middle of the room and motioned for him to sit. He lowered himself into the plastic seat.

"Are you taping this?" He glanced at the two-way mirror behind Janis.

"Of course not. What the hell were you thinking, Ronan?"

"He tried to kill my sister and my..." What was Allison? "He tried to kill us. Fuck! He set my damn house on fire."

She nodded. "Obviously. You look like shit."

He snorted. "Thanks."

"I've been looking into your pal Williams," she said. "Jenson Williams isn't his real name. We ran his prints and found out he's Hugh Davis from up in Young's Cove. Failed a psych eval there and in three other counties. Davis also has a record for assault and battery."

"A real winner, huh?"

She squeezed Ronan's shoulder. "You trusted your gut. I'm impressed."

He shook his head. "I should have figured it out sooner. That fire at Andie's destroyed half the building."

"I know. But you can rest easy tonight." She stood to open the door. "Go home. Let the courts handle Davis."

"Thanks." Ronan gave her a hug. "We'll get coffee and donuts soon."

"Sure thing," she said. "Go get some sleep, huh? You look horrible."

The parking lot was deserted, the night still, when Ronan walked to his truck. He pulled his phone from his pocket and hit the speed dial for Granny. The phone picked up on the first ring.

"Ronan?" Kelly Ann said.

The engine roared to life as he started the truck. "Hey, how are you doing, sis?" he asked.

"We're fine. You coming home?"

"Pulling out of the parking lot now," he said. "Is Diego there?"

"He got here about ten minutes ago," she replied. "Are you sure you're okay?"

"Not a scratch on me," he lied.

"Ronan."

The tremor in her voice twisted his gut. "I promise, Kel. I'm fine. How's Alison? Can I talk to her?"

"She just left."

"Left?" he blurted. "Where did she go?"

"Home."

His heart raced.

Don't blow her leaving out of proportion.

Ronan glanced in the rear-view mirror and made a U-turn. "I'll be home soon," he told Kelly Ann. "Tell Diego to stay there until I get back."

"Where are you going?" Kelly Ann asked.

"I have to check on Alison."

Ronan arrived at the brightly lit, small apartment complex ten minutes later just as a woman got out of a cab. *Alison.* Ronan pulled up in the spot the cab vacated, and the woman's head snapped in his direction. The fear that flashed across her face tore him up inside. Recognition followed, and a different kind of fear widened her eyes. Fuck, he'd been right. She intended to end things between them.

He cut the engine and jumped out of the truck.

"Is everything all right?" she asked. "What are you doing here?"

He stopped beside her. God, he wanted to pull her into his arms and never let her go. "I'm okay. I just wanted to make sure you got home safely. I...I was kind of surprised you left without saying goodbye."

She looked away. "I, well, I have to get back to Emmy."

"Sure." Ronan glimpsed his t-shirt under her open jacket, the shirt's hem hiding the waist of her jeans. The streetlights in front of the complex made her hair shine.

She frowned. "Are you sure you're okay?"

"I'm a little amped up, actually." Ronan let out a deep breath. "Alison, I'm sorry."

"Sorry? Ronan—"

"No." He ran a hand through his hair. "I knew members of the RPFD were being targeted. But I asked you to spend the night because I was scared you would wake up tomorrow and change your mind about me. It was selfish of me to ask you to stay."

She gave a gentle smile. "We had a snowstorm. Staying was the smart choice."

He heard the unspoken words, *But making love wasn't.*

"This wasn't a one-night stand for me," he said. "I'm falling for you."

Surprise flashed in her eyes.

She shivered, and he cursed inwardly. "Come on, let's get you inside."

CHAPTER THIRTY-TWO

Inside? She couldn't let him inside. She could still feel his warm hands, his lips, on her body. If he came inside…

Alison swallowed. He said he was falling for her, but he couldn't know that. Their relationship had been fueled by adrenaline. First, the excitement of New Year's Eve. The fire at the bar…the fire at the house tonight. The life-and-death start to the new year had created an all-too-intense bond. Add the danger of his job to the mix, and their relationship could go up in flames. If she stayed in this relationship and he left, her heart would surely break this time around. Better to end things now.

"Alison."

She froze at the door with her key partway to the lock.

"Please let me come inside," he said behind her. "Just to talk."

She turned. He stood under the pale glow of the streetlight. His messy and tousled hair took her back to earlier in the night when they had made love. His beautiful eyes looked so lost. "Ronan, I need time."

"No, Alison." He ran his hand through his hair. "I will give you anything and everything I have. Even my heart, if you'll take it, but I don't want to give you time to change your mind about us."

Alison hesitated.

"Five minutes," he whispered.

She released a breath. "Five minutes."

She faced the door and Ronan stepped up behind her. She turned the key in the lock and tried to ignore his heat.

Once inside, Ronan paid Alison's neighbor Geri for babysitting before Alison had the chance to remove her wallet from her purse.

"Well, hello," Geri said. "And goodbye."

Alison shuffled her fellow college student to the door. "Thank you for watching Emmy."

"Of course. She slept the whole time," Geri said. She looked at Ronan, widened her eyes, then winked at Alison.

"What?" Alison asked.

Geri motioned her head toward Ronan and gave an exaggerated wink. "Nice."

Alison's heart squeezed. Geri lived for gossip. But there would be nothing to tell after tonight.

"I'm going to check on Emmy," Alison said after she locked the door behind Geri.

Ronan nodded, then slipped his jacket off and tossed it on the sofa.

In her daughter's room, Alison stared down at Emmy. She lay on her side, her little mouth puckered in sleep. Alison pulled the blanket a little more snugly around her shoulders. Emmy meant everything to her. She couldn't be distracted from caring for her—not even by broad shoulders and deep blue eyes. Tonight had been wonderful. Until the fire.

Two fires in one week. Alison shivered. The fires weren't Ronan's fault, but they were a firsthand reminder of what he faced every time he arrived at the scene of a fire.

Her heart clenched. He was brave—far braver than her. Tonight had frightened her more than anything in her life. Not just for herself, Kelly Ann, or the guys, but for Emmy. If anything ever happened to her, Emmy would go to her parents. As much as Alison loved them—as much as her mother tried— she and Alison's stepdad weren't equipped to raise a baby. Emmy needed *her*.

But Alison was safe, and the man who had threatened them was behind bars. She was no longer in danger. Of losing her life, that is. She'd all but lost her heart to Ronan, but he was in danger every time he put on that firefighter's helmet. She wouldn't survive if anything happened to him.

She would never forget the time spent in Ronan's arms, but she had no more to give. She forced back the lump in her throat.

God, she was a hypocrite. She'd told Ronan she wasn't inter- ested in a one-night stand, but that's what tonight had become.

Alison steeled herself. It was late, they were both tired and emotional, but she had to end things before anyone got hurt.

When she walked out of the nursery, she found Ronan looking at the photos on her refrigerator, most of which featured Emmy.

Ronan glanced at her over his shoulder and smiled. "I love this photo." He tugged a photo of her at the beach from the fridge.

Alison took the picture from him and smiled. "I can't fit in this bikini anymore." She once thought that was one of her biggest problems. Now...

"It's the smile on your face."

"I was seventeen," she said. "This was taken before I was married. I was happy."

"You weren't guarded."

Her heart squeezed. He was right. Things weren't that

simple anymore. She stuck the photograph back on the fridge. "I can't be that girl, again. I warned you on New Year's Eve."

"I scared you when I told you I was falling for you, didn't I?"

He had. More than she would have thought possible.

She released a breath. "Tonight was more wonderful than I could've dreamed."

"Don't do this, Alison." He stepped closer. "We have something special."

He was right.

"You deserve someone without all my baggage," she murmured.

"Bullshit," he said, and she couldn't help a little smile.

"It's easy to think differently now. But being a father isn't easy." She met his gaze squarely. "That's the biggest requirement for the man in my life."

He shook his head. "The biggest requirement is being a good man. I've got my faults, but I'm a good man."

Tears pressed the backs of her eyes. "Too good for me."

His eyes widened. "That's not what I said. Stop trying to push me away, Alison. It's not going to work. You've had your heart broken. That doesn't scare me. I don't think you're being honest." She started to reply, but he said, "Sure, you've been hurt, and you have a child to consider, but everything I've seen tells me you follow your heart. I think your heart is telling you that if anything happened to me, you wouldn't be able to recover."

She drew a sharp breath.

He nodded. "I see it in your eyes."

"I have to be here for Emmy," she whispered.

Ronan wrapped his arms around her and pulled her against his chest. She closed her eyes and listened to the strong thump of his heart. He made her feel safer than she'd thought possible.

"You're not going to lose me," he said.

"I can't." Alison pushed away from him. "I'm sorry. I can't."

He stepped toward her. "Alison, I can—"

She retreated. "Please leave."

"I know you care for me."

Her head whirled. "Leave. Please."

He hesitated, eyes pleading. Then he nodded and whirled. She watched as he crossed the room. The door clicked shut before she realized he'd left his coat. She started toward the couch, but got one step and burst into tears.

She stumbled into the living room, dropped back onto the couch and buried her face in his coat.

CHAPTER THIRTY-THREE

The door to *Latte Lunch* opened and a blast of chilled air washed over Alison. She cupped her coffee with both hands and almost moaned at the warmth seeping through her fingers.

She should study at home instead of at this crowded college café—especially since the only seat she'd been able to get had been near the door. God, she was a coward. So what if her apartment was too quiet without Emmy? Isn't quiet what students needed to study?

She glanced at the clock in the lower right-hand corner of her computer. One p.m. Only three more hours until her parents brought Emmy home. She could study for another three hours. She *needed* to study. The assignments were already piling up. But her mind kept wandering back to the hurt on Ronan's face when she'd kicked him out of her apartment three days ago.

Three days. It felt more like minutes. The hurt would lessen. The pain had eventually eased after Levi's betrayal. Still, in some odd way, Ronan was different. This pain brought a sense of frightening finality.

"Excuse me."

Alison started when she realized a young woman stood at her table, hands on the chair across from her.

Alison's cheeks warmed with embarrassment. She tried a casual laugh. "Sorry, my head was in this homework. Did you need something?"

The girl grimaced. "I hate homework."

"We all do," Alison agreed.

"Are you using this chair?" The girl tapped the chair opposite Alison.

"Oh, no," Alison replied. "Take it."

The girl smiled. "Thanks."

She scooted the chair two tables over and sat with three other students. A double-edged pang of envy and loneliness stabbed Alison's chest. She had just started school; in time, she would make friends.

Would that make her forget about Ronan?

A lump formed in her throat. Nothing would make her forget him. It was better—in so many ways—that she had ended things when she had. Ronan was a good guy—but for all his remonstrations, he hadn't tried contacting her again.

Can you blame him?

No. He had respected her wishes and left her alone. Why did that hurt as much as her telling him to leave?

The door opened again and she hunched against the chilling breeze.

"God, you're such an idiot, Alison," she muttered.

"I don't think you're an idiot," a deep male voice said.

Alison jerked around to find Ronan standing inside the door. "What—what are you doing here?"

"Sorry it took me so long to get here," he said. "You know how it is, signing up for classes and all."

"Classes?" she repeated.

He pulled a sheet of paper from his coat pocket, unfolded it, and placed it on the table in front of her:

PURDUE UNIVERSITY GLOBAL
CM107 College Composition I. 5 credits
MM150 Survey of Mathematics 5 credits
SC235 General Biology 5 credits

ALISON LOOKED UP AT HIM. "What is this?"

"The classes I'm taking to get my BA in Fire Science."

She shook her head. "I don't understand."

"I have my Associates, but Marshall O'Malley told me the best way to get a good job as a Fire Inspector is to get my Bachelors."

Was this really happening?

He squatted so that his face was level with hers. "Did you think I would give up so easily?"

"I—" She shook her head.

He gave her a gentle smile. "I know my work frightens you. Hell, it's frightened Kelly Ann from day one. My grandmother too, I suspect, but she won't say so."

"You need someone better than me," she whispered.

Ronan stood and pulled her into his arms. He held her so tight she almost couldn't breathe.

He pressed his mouth against her ear. "Don't tell me what I need, Alison. Unless you're telling me that someone is you."

Her heart pounded.

"Do you care about me?" His warm breath washed over her ear. "Even a little?"

She could only nod against his chest.

"That's a start," the relief in his voice caught her off guard.

"I care about you *and* Emmy," he said. "I want to be there for you both."

Tears stung the corners of her eyes. He leaned back, but she kept her eyes downcast. God, she couldn't let him see her cry. With a finger beneath her chin, he tilted her head up so that she was forced to look at him, and he gently wiped away her tears with a thumb.

Alison shook her head. "I can't ask you to give up the work you love."

"You didn't." His expression sobered. "This decision has been a long time coming. You were the kick in the ass I needed to finally admit what I wanted all along." His eyes darkened. "Think you would date a fire inspector instead of a firefighter?"

Unexpected shyness washed over her. "Is he cute?"

He lifted one arm and flexed his bicep. "You tell me."

"Too sexy," she said.

He pulled her against his chest. "I'll have to work until a position opens up. Can you live with that?"

"Yes," she whispered.

He yanked her against him and kissed her so hard her head spun.

Applause filled the crowded café.

Ronan winked. "Whatever you do, don't tell your firefighter boyfriend that you're dating a college student. I hear those firefighters protect their own."

Her mouth went dry. "Am I yours?"

"You and Emmy both," he said in a husky tone.

She had thought her dating life was over after becaming a mom. She had turned her back on men based on her past. But Ronan hadn't given up on her. He had shown her his dedication to her and her daughter. He had opened his heart to them both.

Alison threw her arms around his neck and ignored a second round of applause as she kissed him.

EPILOGUE

Two Years Later

"YOU'VE NEVER LOOKED SO sexy, Mama." Ronan looked down at his beautiful wife and their newborn daughter asleep in her arms.

"We both know that isn't true." Alison gave him a tired smile before she dropped her head on his shoulder. He wasn't supposed to be in bed with her—hospital policy—but nothing could keep them apart.

"You're a superstar, baby." He kissed the top of her head. "Fifteen hours of labor."

"You owe me for that."

Ronan laughed. "You want a foot rub?"

"Later. I just want to hold her."

"Our sweet little Alana," Ronan said.

Alison pressed a kiss to Ronan's neck. "Emmy loves her."

Ronan laughed. "She didn't want to leave with your parents."

"I didn't want her to leave," Alison said. "But I'm really tired. Take Alana, hubs."

Ronan took his newborn daughter from Alison and cradled her in his arm. "She feels lighter than seven pounds."

"Funny how I gained thirty." Alison set her hand on his chest. "I'm just going to say Happy New Year now, Ronan. There's no guarantee I'll make it to midnight."

"Sleep, honey. I'll wake you for my kiss."

Alison's eyes closed. "This is much more low key than last year."

"Andie's grand re-opening." Ronan smiled at the memory. "And the night I proposed."

"On stage in front of a bar full of disappointed women," Alison said. "It was perfect. New Year's Eve is special to us."

"Not quite as special as March twenty-eighth."

"Our wedding day." Alison reached over to caress her daughter's cheek. "Our honeymoon baby."

"I'm so happy, Alison. To have you, Emmy, and now little Alana in my life." Ronan smiled. "My three girls."

"I'm glad you were able to take the day off work," Alison said around a yawn.

"O'Malley loves me. She gives me anything I ask for."

They laughed at his lie. Ronan didn't have the best relationship with his new boss at the Fire Marshal's office, but he'd stuck it out this past year because of his passion for the job.

"How do you think the calendar party is going tonight?" Alison asked. "Do you miss firefighting?"

"Yes and no. There are days I miss the excitement of a call," Ronan said, "but I love being an investigator. No regrets."

"Even though you weren't eligible to pose for the charity calendar this year?"

His laughter made Alana squirm, but, thankfully, she didn't wake. "I think that might be the best part of the new job."

"Kelly Ann will tell us all about it tomorrow, when she and Diego come meet Alana."

Ronan nodded. "Hopefully, he didn't propose to her tonight."

"They're waiting until she's finished college. Don't stress, big brother." Alison dropped her head back onto the pillow. "I'm tired."

"Sleep, my love." Ronan stood and laid their sleeping daughter in the plastic bassinette beside the bed. "I'll go get us some chocolate from the vending machine."

"I love you for that."

Ronan walked into the waiting room, fed change into the vending machine, and decided on two Kit Kat bars. He checked his phone and noticed a couple missed calls from the bar. Ronan retrieved the candy, then dialled Joey.

"Happy New Year, Daddy," Joey answered.

Ronan laughed. "Thanks. Happy New Year."

"How are the girls?" Joey asked.

"Tired, but we're so damn happy. Alison was a star, and Alana is sleeping."

"Megan went crazy over the photo you sent," Joey said. "Alana's a little doll."

"That she is. How are the calendar boys?" Ronan asked.

"Good, good. The new rookie, Sam, is a hit." Joey laughed. "But I think you're missed on stage."

"Well, I'm right where I need to be tonight."

"That you are. Megan and I just wanted to congratulate you again."

"We appreciate it."

"When will you be home from the hospital?"

"We'll be released in the morning. Kelly Ann is bringing up a going home outfit for Alana." Ronan laughed. "Should be interesting."

"Sounds great. Give Alison our love, okay?"

"Will do. Happy New Year."

Ronan slid his phone into his pocket and headed back to see his girls.

He reached Alison's room and was surprised to find her sitting up, feeding Alana. He sat beside her and watched his daughter. "Joey and Megan called to wish you a Happy New Year."

"Aw. I love them."

Ronan kissed Alison's cheek. "Can you believe two years have come and gone since we met?"

"Life has only gotten better since," she said.

"I married a college girl," he said with a wink. "I adopted Emmy, I have great in-laws, best friends. A job I love."

"And a new baby," Alison said. "She's going to be a daddy's girl, like Emmy."

"Alana Joy."

Alison smiled. "Your mom would be honored we're using her name."

He nodded. "Mom would have loved you and our girls."

Her eyes shimmered with unshed tears. "I wish I could give her back to you. Your father, too."

His chest tightened.

Alison cupped his cheek with one hand. "I love you so much, Mr. July."

He thought about the last two years of his life: picnics with Emmy, dinners with Gran. He and Alison hoisting up the chili cookoff trophy. Two years running. Their wedding and honeymoon. His first day on the job at the fire marshal's office. This morning, holding Alison's hand as she gave birth to their newest daughter.

"I love you, Alison McGuire."

She lifted a brow. "So, was our first kiss worth five hundred dollars?"

Ronan grinned and pulled her and their daughter close. "Oh, hell yeah."

SNEAK PEEK AT ABDUCTED

TEXAS RANGERS: SPECIAL OPS
RECONNAISSANCE TEAM

TARAH SCOTT AND EVAN TREVANE

He's too hot, too smart, and too young...and too damn hard to resist.

The El Paso fashion gala was slated to be the hottest event of the year and a must do if Liz Monahan, the creative brains behind Nina Bruno Designs, was to vault the company to the big time. Circumstances put Liz at the party in one of her own creations, escorted by a young, handsome model hired to show her off to the well-known and well-established. But Liz didn't count on her date being an undercover Texas Ranger who is investigating a human trafficking ring. She also didn't count on being kidnapped and trafficked herself.

When Texas Ranger Ben Hunter slips away from Liz Monahan at the gala and begins his investigation, he couldn't be more surprised to arrive in Juarez, Mexico to find her held captive by infamous human trafficker Carlos Sanchez. In order to save her, Ben must commit murder. Hers.

Nina Bruno Designs caters to the modern woman. The mature woman who knows that life begins after forty.

Liz mentally repeated the litany as she blinked at the strobe of photoflashes illuminating the night outside the limousine. The car slowed behind a line of other limos entering a circular drive and Francis Remmey's estate came into full view. Spotlights crisscrossed the Edwardian columns and stone façade of the mansion.

Only a few hours ago, she had been giddy at the prospect of getting caught on camera by the reporters that now crowded each approaching vehicle and lined both sides of the walkway leading to the hacienda's steps. It seemed the entire state of Texas had converged on El Paso for the fashion event of the year, the fifth annual *G International Gala* hosted by Larissa Remmey, owner of *G International* fashion magazine.

Now, however, getting noticed was a double-edged sword.

Liz shifted her attention to the two co-workers sitting across from her. Richard Anderson, VP of Marketing of Nina Bruno Designs, and Brenda Pierce, Head Designer.

"This is a bad idea," Liz said.

"You and your dress are going to be a hit," Richard said. "Stop worrying."

The knot in her stomach cinched tighter. "What in God's name were we thinking? We have an arsenal of models, any of whom would pant at the opportunity to debut the first design in our winter collection. Just because Lisa wasn't able to accept our offer to replace Tanya didn't mean we couldn't find someone else. Why didn't we try?"

"Name someone else who lives in El Paso," Richard said. "Even better, name someone old enough who would fit into that dress. You're the one who's been selling the idea that older women don't want to see teenagers modeling the clothes they buy."

Liz tugged the bustier top higher. She had to remember to make the darts deeper for women her size. "My *attributes* aren't enough to warrant me modeling this dress."

"Yes, they are," he replied. "But the point is moot. We had no choice."

Liz tamped down on the panic that began three hours ago upon watching the news report that their New York buyer Genevra had declared bankruptcy. That meant the three hundred thousand dollar payment they were expecting in sixty days wasn't coming. An hour after they'd learned about Genevra, they got a call from a local reporter that the model they'd hired to debut their winter-line dress had just been seen getting into a limo outside her downtown El Paso hotel wearing a layered chiffon flamenco-style dress that screamed Jorge Estonia—their direct competition in Dallas.

In a span of three hours, Nina Bruno Designs—the company she had poured her life savings into—had gone from the verge of financial independence to teetering on financial ruin. The worst part was that the employees and investors now expected her to pull off what Tanya could have accomplished in her sleep.

When Brenda had approached Liz with the design early that spring, she'd fallen in love with the strapless, bustier-style leather bodice and chic gathered skirt design. But the thought never entered her mind that she might be forced to wear the twenty-seven inch dress in an effort to keep the company from going under.

Another Xenon-flash flared, jarring her from her thoughts.

Brenda leaned forward and straightened the strap on Liz's three-inch heel sandal. "You look as good as Tanya in that dress."

Liz pursed her lips. "We promoted Tanya as the model for this dress. People are expecting her, not a replacement ten years older, and certainly not a company executive."

"You're only seven years older," Richard said. "But you don't look a day over her thirty-seven."

Liz shot him a dry look. "If that's meant to boost my ego, it doesn't."

Richard returned the look. "Get your priorities straight, Liz. You want our first invitation to Larissa's gala to be our last? Without this event, our winter collection ends up in bargain stores and we don't get invited to another major fashion show this year."

Liz knew he really meant, 'We won't be in a position to go to another major fashion show this year—maybe no other fashion show ever.' The company no longer had the luxury of growing slowly. This was Nina Bruno Designs' only chance to stay in business.

"Damn that bitch," he muttered.

"Richard," Liz admonished.

He shook his head. "Don't start with me. You hired Tanya."

"She's the best model in her age bracket," Liz said. "And, as you pointed out, one of the few who would fit into this dress."

His eyes lowered to her chest. "Not anymore."

FROM THE CORNER of his eye, Ben saw another limo stop in front of the estate and turned his head in time to see the rear door open and Richard Anderson emerge from the vehicle. Anderson turned and extended a hand into the car's open doorway. A slim arm reached toward him and cameras flashed in quick succession as a long, shapely leg stretched toward the paving stones. Elizabeth Monahan's face came into view, illuminated by camera lights.

Ben lifted an eyebrow in appreciation as she rose to her full five foot nine—no, he dropped his attention to her three-inch heels—her six-foot *height*. He raised his gaze up those long legs, then the pleated skirt that brushed toned thighs, and blew out a silent whistle. *Whoa.* Her breasts nearly spilled over the bodice of the leather top—the dress that was kicking off the winter collection for Nina Bruno. His appreciative mood vanished. What was the Creative Director of Nina Bruno Designs doing wearing the dress Tanya Xavier—his date—was supposed to be modeling?

NB Designs had hired him as Tanya's escort. He was the arm candy that said, *Buy this dress and land a man like me.*

Something had gone wrong for Elizabeth Monahan to be wearing the main attraction. Was he to escort her or did the change of plans include another escort? Maybe she decided that Tanya would wear another dress. He didn't like surprises. She should have called. But why would she? He was just the hired help.

Richard Anderson slipped Ms. Monahan's hand into the crook of his arm and led her toward the steps. Toward Ben. She glanced left, and the press snapped photos and thrust microphones toward her. Then she spotted him. Her brow furrowed. Understanding hardened her expression and Ben read in her eyes a mirror image of his thoughts: *What the hell are you doing here?* He'd bet a thousand bucks someone forgot to call him to cancel. Damn good thing, too, because he'd have come no matter what.

They reached him.

"This isn't going to work," Elizabeth hissed under her breath.

She had that right. Was that a hint of nipple peeking over the bodice of her dress? The damn thing was scandalous, even for these over-the-top designers.

"You knew Adam was going to be here, Liz," Richard said in a low voice. "You hired him."

Adam Billings. His alias.

She flashed a dazzling smile that caught Ben off guard before he caught sight of a reporter pointing a camera at them. The camera flashed and her smile didn't falter when she said under her breath to Anderson, "You know good-and-well I forgot he was going to be here, and you conveniently forgot to remind me."

She darted a glance over her shoulder, clearly worried her whispered words might have been overheard by a reporter who had edged closer. Not much chance of that happening amid the babble of other reporters.

She really couldn't ask him to leave, but he had to play the part of a pliant employee. Ben angled his head away from the reporters in case any of the vultures could read lips. "I can leave, if you prefer, ma'am."

"Liz, half of Texas is watching us," Anderson said. "Make a

scene now, and it'll be all over the state before the evening is over. We need him."

Something Ben couldn't quite define flickered in her gaze, then she shot Anderson a look to kill. "I sleep with the CEO, Richard. You're fired."

Ben bit back a laugh.

Anderson nodded. "Sure thing, Liz. As soon as the party's over, I'll pack up my desk." He transferred her hand to Ben's arm. "She's all yours. Good luck."

The determination to get to know her better had formed two days ago, during a photo shoot with him and Tanya after the Thompson Agency sent him in to replace the model originally hired to escort Tanya.

Ben glanced at her legs, then reminded himself not to combine business with pleasure. So what if he hadn't expected to see her tonight dressed in an outfit that heated his blood? He had to get inside the Remmey's mansion. Business now. Pleasure later.

Liz gripped his arm and he had the feeling she was considering a quick getaway. Ben covered her hand with his—if nothing else to keep her from bolting. Liz Monahan was his ticket through the door.

He led her up the stairs and a man dressed like a British soldier opened the door at their approach. They entered the foyer and the door closed behind them, cutting off the voices. Ben squinted against a glow of chandelier light bouncing off the white marble floor. A sweeping staircase to their right led to a gallery that encircled the foyer. Directly ahead, three arched doorways opened to the rear of the estate. An escape route if anything went wrong. But Liz Monahan as his date might ensure nothing went wrong. Slipping away from her would be easier than ditching Tanya. If Liz was all business as she had been during their shoot two days ago, she wouldn't miss him.

He steered her left, toward the music wafting through an arched doorway. They reached the room and he turned Liz right in the direction of a dancefloor near a twelve-piece orchestra.

Ben waited until they'd passed a man and woman talking in low tones before whispering to her, "Is that true?"

She looked up. "What?"

He leaned closer. "Do you really sleep with the CEO?"

Frustration flickered across her features. "No, but I'd give him a go if he really would fire Richard."

Ben laughed. He just bet she would. "He's right, you know. You are the one who hired me."

Her eyes narrowed. "*You* I *can* fire—and don't think your good looks will stop me."

So she had noticed. During the photo shoot she'd appraised him like a prize horse.

Ben shrugged. "I'm an independent contractor, if you recall. I don't have to work for Nina Bruno Designs again."

"Nina Bruno Designs is the best designer this side of the Mississippi. You'd be a fool not to want to work for us again."

She actually sounded offended.

"Maybe that means I should sleep with *you*," he said.

She shot him one of the looks she'd given Anderson. "I don't rob the cradle."

"Then I guess we have a deal."

She opened her mouth for a retort but, instead, smiled at a large group they skirted a large group

"Not that I'm disappointed," he said, "but where is Tanya, by the way?"

She slowed and her smile wavered. "Over there."

He looked across the sea of bodies in the direction she stared. Tanya stood surrounded by a group of men. The man on her left shifted so that his face came into view and Ben's heart jumped to a hard hammer.

Carlos Sanchez.

The human traffics dealer wasn't supposed to be in Texas.

LIZ STOOD STOCK STILL UNTIL TANYA'S ATTENTION CAUGHT on her. The model's gaze flicked to Liz's dress, then her eyes swung back to her face in wide-eyed surprise.

"She seems surprised to see you—or to see you wearing that dress," Adam whispered.

So he'd noticed that, too. Liz, Richard, and Brenda had been so consumed with finding a replacement for Tanya that they automatically concluded she jilted them because Jorge offered her more money. Tanya's reaction, however, suggested something else. She hadn't expected to see the dress at all.

Disbelief turned to fury. Tanya hadn't dumped them for a better offer. She had sabotaged them.

"She decided to play for another team at the last moment, didn't she?" Adam said.

Liz snapped her gaze up to meet his. His attention shifted from the couple to her. She thought she discerned tension in his jaw, but it wasn't there now and he lifted a brow.

"By the look on your face, I'd say I'm right. Who's the competition?" he asked.

Liz hesitated, but realized the news of Tanya's defection

was likely scheduled for the next print run of every gossip column in Texas. "Jorge Designs."

"Is that who she's with?"

Liz shifted her attention to Tanya's escort. He was tall, early forties, absolutely gorgeous, with jet black hair and honey brown eyes. The poster boy for the South American gigolo.

"Not Jorge Estonia," she murmured aloud. "And he's too old to be a model."

"So are you."

Liz cut Adam a narrow-eyed glance. "You really know how to sweet talk your boss."

He shrugged. "I'm not the one who said a woman isn't attractive after twenty-five."

"You'll likely think differently when you reach thirty."

He smiled and her heart skipped a beat. His smile could stop traffic. Suddenly, she wondered if she'd been going about selling clothes the wrong way. This man was a dynamite package. His blue eyes smoldered—a stunning combination enhanced by his black tux. Six-foot-four of pure male. No contacts, no drug-induced biceps, just good old-fashioned Mother Nature at her ever-loving best. But despite his looks, it was his smile that truly set him apart from the other models. It didn't matter who wore the dress, only that when a woman wore it, this man would smile at them.

"Why didn't you smile like that for the photo shoot?" Liz asked.

Amusement lit his eyes. "Now that I know you like my smile, I'll be sure to do it more often."

Liz nodded. "You're going to sell my dress for me."

"That's what I'm here for. But you don't give yourself enough credit. You're going to give Tanya a run for her money." He leaned closer and his warm breath brushed her ear as he whispered, "What do you say we go on the offensive and say hello to her and her date?"

Liz imagined Adam's full mouth pressed against her ear. She jarred from the thought. Good Lord, the man was sixteen years her junior—and she was his boss. And he was staring expectantly.

"What?" she blurted.

A very young female model on the arm of a high school graduate slowed as they passed, and Liz realized her outburst had caught their attention. Liz became aware she was squeezing Adam's bicep and started to pull away.

He covered her hand with his. "Nope," he said. "We have to look like we can't live without each other."

Liz glanced down at his hand on hers. The light scratch of calluses against the top of her hand surprised her. Odd. Most male models were as big a prima donna as their female counterparts and seldom lifted a finger for fear a drop of sweat would spoil their looks. But Adam had a down-to-earth quality. Yet tonight, he exuded a dangerous edge that hadn't been present during the photo shoot.

She glanced at Tanya, who had turned her back and was speaking with a group of people. Tanya clutched her date's arm, and Liz knew she was sending a signal: I don't need Nina Bruno Designs.

She would regret that decision.

A waiter passed in front of Liz. Adam released her and snagged two glasses of champagne. He handed one to Liz. She took a large swig. A woman at least sixty years of age raked her gaze down Adam's body. He seemed not to notice and slipped an arm around Liz's waist. Warmth spread through her stomach. Champagne did that to a person. Her second drink nearly emptied the glass.

Liz spotted Larissa Remmey just as the woman turned and

met her gaze. The older woman's eyes lit. Attention fixed on Liz, she said something to the man on her right, then started across the room.

Liz smiled and kept her gaze on Larissa as she whispered to Adam, "You get me through this night and there's a bonus in it for you."

"Is it the bonus we discussed earlier?"

"Earlier—" She jerked her gaze onto his face. "I told you, I don't rob the cradle, nor do I mix business with pleasure. Understand?"

"Yes, ma'am," he drawled. "No business with pleasure. I'll be sure to keep them separate."

Liz blinked and wondered whether he had noticed her reaction to him a moment ago. Dammit, she had no one but herself to blame for that. Before she could say more, Larissa reached them and extended her arms.

"Darling," she said with the barest hint of a Russian accent.

Liz shot Adam a quelling look as Larissa pulled her into a cheek hug.

———

BEN KEPT HIS EXPRESSION CASUAL. He didn't typically like surprises, but Liz Monahan as his date and Texas' most wanted human traffics dealer showing up in El Paso tonight were two surprises he could live with. It looked like he wasn't going to have to go snooping around the Remmey's mansion, after all, to discover their connection to Carlos Sanchez. He could go straight to Sanchez. If he could get the man alone.

Liz slipped her hand through the crook of Ben's arm. Before he could corner Sanchez, he'd have to slip away from Liz Monahan. He shifted his attention and found himself staring straight down her cleavage. He jerked his gaze up as Larissa said, "So this is the dress we've all been waiting to see." The older woman nodded approval.

Liz laughed, low and sensual, and Ben's groin surprised him by giving a hard salute. He hadn't been this intensely affected when he'd met Laura five years ago. He'd been crazy about her, had even considered marriage. But after two years of dating, he still wasn't home enough to ask her to marry into an empty house, and she simply fell out of love with him.

Staying closer to home won't be a problem with Liz.

The thought brought him up short. He'd thought about her a lot these last two days, but when had he decided he wanted to spend more time at home with a woman? Liz released his arm and Ben resisted the impulse to grasp her hand and put it back. Tonight was about business—for both of them—and he couldn't afford to let her get in his way.

"I doubt you've been waiting all season to see a Nina Bruno design," she said to Larissa.

"On the contrary," Larissa replied. "Your lineup last year was impressive. I've been watching you, as have others. I'm intrigued by the fact you chose to wear the debut dress yourself. Very bold. The leather top fits you to perfection—or I should say, you fill it out to perfection."

Pink tinged Liz's cheeks. "We use the gifts given us," she said.

"And why not?" Larissa said. She turned to Ben. "And who is this luscious thing?"

"Mrs. Remmey, meet Adam Billings," Liz said. "Adam—"

"No introductions are necessary," he cut in. "It's a pleasure to meet you, Mrs. Remmey."

Larissa's eyes lit with pleasure. "Ohh, a charmer." She stepped closer and curved her fingers around his arm. "I think you'll be my pet for the evening."

"Pet for the evening?" a female voice said.

Even as Ben registered the familiar voice, the speaker stepped into view. He froze. The last person he expected to see was Assistant DA Sheila Antonio. He couldn't allow her to discover that Carlos Sanchez occupied the same room with her.

Ben snapped from a brain freeze and said, "You're Sheila Antonio." He extended a hand. "Adam Billings. I'm a big fan."

Her brows lifted in an expression of polite curiosity. She slid her hand into his and gave a hard squeeze, intended to remind him of their last encounter.

He felt the curious gazes of Liz and Mrs. Remmey and flashed his most charming grin. "You made big news last year when you prosecuted that drug dealer the Border Patrol caught with two kilos of cocaine. The guy put out a hit on you, but that didn't stop you from putting him away for twenty years."

"Not Border Patrol," Sheila said. "The Texas Rangers caught him."

"What's the difference?"

"There's a world of difference." A glint appeared in her eyes. "They didn't catch the man contracted to kill me."

They weren't supposed to. He was the hitman, and she knew it.

"Isn't he delicious?" Mrs. Remmey interjected.

Sheila nodded. "Yes, he is."

"But he's spoken for." Mrs. Remmey glanced at Liz. "You don't mind, do you, darling?"

"My escort is your escort," Liz replied.

Ben glanced at Sanchez. The man laughed at something another guest said. Ben had to break free of the women. He couldn't chance Sanchez leaving the party.

"We'll talk later, Sheila," Mrs. Remmey said. "I have to show off Liz to my other guests."

"It was very nice to meet you, Ms. Antonio," Ben said.

She inclined her head. "Perhaps we'll have a chance to talk more later?"

"I wouldn't count on it," Mrs. Remmey said. "I plan to keep him to myself." She started away and Ben turned his attention to her. "Come along, Liz," she said. "I believe tonight is going to be your lucky night."

www.scarsdalepublishing.com

www.ingramcontent.com/pod-product-compliance
Lightning Source LLC
Chambersburg PA
CBHW021329190726
48288CB00003B/1025